PAW PRINTS AND PROBLEMS

A TALKING DOG COZY MYSTERY

HEYWOOD HOUNDS COZY MYSTERIES
BOOK TWO

CARLY WINTER

Edited by
DIVAS AT WORK EDITING
Cover By
COVEREDBYMELINDA.COM

WESTWARD PUBLISHING / CARLY FALL, LLC

ABOUT THIS BOOK

A dead chef is bad for business... and so is being accused of murder.

When restaurant owner, Sally Turner, finds her chef murdered, she realizes she's in deep trouble... especially when she was the last one to see the victim alive and they'd been arguing when she left him. She turns to Gina for help in finding the real killer.

As Gina assists Deputy Trevor Hutchison exploration into the chef's past, they find a cast of unsavory characters, lies and danger. Amidst the investigation, an unexpected guest - a rambunctious golden retriever named Zeus - lands on Gina's doorstep. Juggling the search for a murderer and managing the mischievous canine tests Gina's patience, leading to conflict with those around her.

With her talking dog, Daisy, at her side, will Gina be able to find the destructive Zeus a suitable home and navigate the investigation without becoming a victim herself?

PREVIOUSLY IN THE HEYWOOD HOUNDS COZY MYSTERIES...

In Dog Treats and Death:

When Gina Dunner's brother, Vic, is accused of murdering his ex-girlfriend, Gina isn't surprised. Living the life of a womanizing ranch hand with questionable friends and a lifetime of bad choices had to catch up with him at some point.

After the Sheriff announces she has the right man, Vic vehemently denies the murder. When he begs Gina to help prove his innocence, she attempts to puts her doubts aside, despite him being the last one to see the woman alive. She and her rescue mutt, Daisy—a sweet, yet sassy, talking dog—start sniffing around into their own investigation.

CHAPTER 1

AS SUMMER FADED and fall slowly moved in, the leaves on the trees along the river in Heywood began to turn beautiful shades of red, yellow and orange. Although I'd lived in the small mountain town my whole life, I never tired of seeing them and each year I was awestruck by their beauty.

Even in this early morning hour. The only reason I was up was because Daisy, my talking dog, had woken me, claiming it was the perfect time for a walk. While glancing around at nature's beauty, I realized she hadn't been wrong.

Daisy and I strolled along the Riverwalk in the crisp morning hours, with her chatting incessantly about a cat we'd seen earlier while I admired the trees and thought about my day. I had completed the murder mystery book and turned it in to the author, who had loved it and commissioned another one. I had no plot, so my mind seemed to continuously spin with ideas, as well as a myriad of plot holes.

"I think that cat wanted to eat me," Daisy said. "Either that or beat me up. He was not a nice cat."

The feline had come out from behind a bush, then hissed and snarled at us. Daisy barked, and the two engaged in a standoff until I finally pulled her leash and we moved past it. I assumed the cat to be feral, so I debated whether to call a rescue organization or not. I didn't take in cats, but others in the area did. However, the animal had looked very well fed and healthy, so perhaps he was simply out and about for a morning stroll, just like us.

My phone buzzed in my pocket, and I pulled it out. Sally from On The River. What in the world could she want? We were friends, but we rarely spoke on the phone.

"Hi, Sally," I said. "What's up?"

"Gina?" she sniffled. "I'm sorry, I don't know who else to call."

"What's wrong?" I asked as dread weighed on my chest. "Are you crying?"

"I came in to open the restaurant," she whispered. "And... and one of my workers is dead."

"Who is it?"

"One of my chefs. Mario."

I stopped walking, furrowing my brow. "Well, you may want to call an ambulance," I said. "Maybe he isn't dead. Maybe he had a heart attack or something."

"No, he was murdered, Gina. He's got my favorite knife sticking out of his chest."

"Oh, my word," I gasped. "Have you called the police?"

"Yes. They're here now."

"You need a lawyer," I said. "And you need to keep your mouth shut. Call Colin Breckshire. He can find someone to represent you."

A local lawyer older than dirt with a panache for bowties and fedoras, Colin was the closest thing to a criminal attorney this area had. Maybe that needed to change.

"It's too late."

"What does that mean?" I asked.

"I was nervous... I told the sheriff that it was my favorite knife and that I'd had an argument with him before I left last night, and I was the last to see him alive."

My heart sank as anxiety twisted my stomach. I needed to sit down. Daisy was still prattling on about the cat. My lovely morning had turned ugly.

"Please come help me, Gina. I'm really

afraid of what's going to happen. They keep asking me all these questions... I'm scared they're going to pin this on me like they did to Vic about Phoebe's death."

A few months ago, my brother, Vic, had been accused of murdering his ex-girlfriend. Sheriff Mallory Richards had been ready to arrest him, but he'd hidden out at my house until I could find the real killer. Or, I should say, the real killer had found me. I'd almost ended up becoming one of his victims.

I shut my eyes and rubbed my hand over my forehead. No way was I allowing my friend to take the fall for her dead chef's murder.

I'd simply have to find who did it myself. "I'll be there shortly," I muttered, then hung up and shoved the phone back into my coat pocket.

"You'll be where?" Daisy asked, glancing up at me with her sweet brown gaze. "And when? What does shortly mean? Are we on our way to wherever you said you'd be going? And what about the cat?"

My dog often reminded me of my son, Jacob, when he was young and asked a thousand questions a day. I leaned over and scratched her brown and white head. "We're heading to On The River," I explained. "It seems like Sally is in a bit of trouble."

"Why? What did she do?"

I sighed and glanced around at the trees and the river, trying to recreate that euphoric feeling the beauty had brought me. It was hard, considering there was a dead body just up the Riverwalk in Sally's restaurant. "I think she may be accused of doing something she *didn't* do."

"Like what?" Daisy asked. "Like when that rescue chewed up your slipper but you blamed me?"

As a dog rescuer, I had a revolving door of homeless mutts. More than one had chewed up my slipper, so I had no idea which one she meant. "Yes. Exactly like that."

"So she's innocent and someone thinks she's guilty," Daisy continued.

"Yes."

"Well, why doesn't she just tell them that she didn't do anything?"

"I think she already did, and people don't believe her."

"If I couldn't speak to you, you'd never believe that I didn't chew your slipper," she sniffed.

"You looked guilty," I said. "You were the only one in the bedroom and you were lying with it under your chin."

"I was trying to protect it for you from that beast!"

With a sigh, I shook my head. I still wasn't sure I believed her or not, but it had happened months ago, so it seemed pointless to argue about it.

"Let's head to On The River," I said. "Hopefully, no one has arrested Sally yet."

We hurried down to the end of the path. Thankfully, the gaggle of geese that usually sat on the grassy area had left when the weather had cooled. Oftentimes, they liked to chase Daisy. I found it amusing, but she didn't.

After hiking up the trail to Comfort Road, the main thoroughfare through Heywood, we walked down the street to find a couple of sheriff's vehicles parked in front of the restaurant.

They wouldn't be happy to see me, but I decided to go in anyway.

"Be quiet once we're inside," I whispered to Daisy before opening the door. "I want to take a look around without the cops seeing me."

I cracked the door and took in the scene. The large space reminded me of a cozy log cabin with a large fireplace and pictures of Heywood lining the walls. Two cops stood facing the window on the far side of the restaurant. I recognized the bulk of Deputy Trevor

Hutchison, and casually knew the other guy but couldn't remember his name. Sally was seated in a booth by the doorway leading to the kitchen, her head resting in her hands.

She'd said Sheriff Mallory Richards was also present, but I didn't notice the worthless leader anywhere.

After slipping inside, I took a few steps and attempted to take in more details of the scene. Moving to my left a bit, I now realized the cops were studying the victim, who lay on top of a table, the hilt of a knife sticking out of his chest. Would Sally be strong enough to stab a man so he landed on top of a table? It would seem to me that one would have to hold down the victim, then jam the knife in his chest. Otherwise, wouldn't he fold forward?

Granted, I'd never stabbed anyone, so I was guessing. They always curled forward on television, though.

As I moved farther to the left, I noted there had been a significant struggle from the door of the kitchen to where the victim lay. Broken glass and napkins littered the floor. Was the kitchen also trashed?

I studied Sally. Her shoulders shook silently as she cried. She wore a sleeveless shirt and a sweater sat balled up at her side on the seat. The pale skin on her arms didn't hold a mark.

Based on the wreckage, I imagined she'd have scratches and cuts if she'd been in a struggle with the chef before his demise.

"She didn't do this," I whispered to my dog. "If Mallory tries to pin it on her, I'm going to be really angry."

"We'll go into super sleuth mode and find the real killer!" Daisy yelled. Thankfully, I was the only one who heard her, or our cover would've been blown.

I crouched down behind a table and listened intently.

"Have you called his wife?" Trevor asked.

"Yes," the other deputy responded. "I asked her to meet us at the office."

"What's the wife's name?"

I heard pages turning, as if the man was flipping through a notebook. "Whitney," he replied. "Whitney Maven."

"Don't let Mallory tell you it's not important to talk to her," Trevor said. "Rather than railroading Sally as Mallory indicated she wanted to do, I'd prefer to do a thorough investigation."

"But she was the last one to see him alive and she admitted they had an argument," the deputy said.

"And none of that matters," Trevor rebuked. "It doesn't mean she killed him."

"Yeah, dummy dork dude," Daisy said, her tail wagging as she licked my face. "That's what he is, right, Gina? A dummy dork dude."

"If you say so," I whispered.

"Hey, Sally?" Trevor called. "Are you okay?"

"No, I'm not, Trevor. My chef is dead. My restaurant is trashed, and Mallory actually suggested I was responsible."

He sighed. "Look, let's take this from the top, okay? Can you tell me who would want him dead?"

"I don't know," she said. "We didn't socialize. He was my employee, and I believe boundaries are important in business."

"Did he argue with anyone here at work?" Trevor asked.

"Not that I ever saw. He came to work, cooked great food and left. He was quiet."

My knees became sore from squatting, so I sat down on the floor. When my butt hit the carpet, I hoped the thump wouldn't be heard by anyone else.

"You've got a noisy rear end," Daisy said. "But not as noisy as mine!" She passed gas and laughed hysterically while I tried not to faint from the smell. Placing my hand over my nose and mouth while fighting to breathe, I shot her a glare.

Just then, the front door flew open and a woman came running in. Thin with long black hair, she screamed, "Mario!"

"Uh oh," Daisy said.

The woman was so upset she didn't see us, nor did she smell the foulness Daisy had let loose. "Mario! It's not true!"

"Mrs. Maven?" Trevor asked.

"We told you to meet us at the station!" the second deputy yelled. "This is an active crime scene!"

She continued to scream. I imagined her trying to reach her husband, but the police holding her back. Footsteps sounded from my left and I glanced up to see Sally walking towards us. Daisy's tail wagged as she yelled, "Sally! Hi, Sally! Do you have treats for me?"

Sally shot me a confusing glare, but continued past us.

"Whitney, I'm so sorry for your loss," she said. She must've walked around the restaurant to keep from contaminating the murder scene. "Come over here and sit down."

"Over here?" Daisy asked. "Like by us?"

I scooted under the table and dragged Daisy with me, just in case she was right. Thankfully, Sally had the wherewithal to take a table away from us, but not too close to the body.

"She needs to leave!" the unknown deputy yelled. "Right now!"

"Just give her a minute," Trevor countered. "She's upset."

Heavy breathing filled the air and I assumed the poor woman was hyperventilating.

"I wish we could see what's happening," Daisy said. "I don't like being under this table."

Long moments passed. Sally fetched her a glass of water, once again walking right past us. Finally, Whitney calmed down and Trevor asked, "Mrs. Maven, do you know who would want to kill your husband?"

She began crying once again. "That's not his real name."

"Excuse me?" Trevor replied.

"Mario Maven... that's not his real name."

CHAPTER 2

DAISY and I exchanged glances while she tilted her head to the side and perked her ears. "Why would he go by Mario Maven if that's not his real name?" Daisy asked.

Great question. I brought my finger to my lips so we could listen.

"If Mario Maven wasn't his name, then what was it?" Trevor asked.

"Peter Smith," she sniffed. "Can I get another tissue?"

After Whitney blew her nose, Sally asked, "Why the name change?"

"He... he didn't want people to know his real name or look into his past."

"Why is that?" Trevor questioned.

"Because he was in prison."

A heavy silence fell over the room as the truth permeated the air.

"This is getting good," Daisy murmured while Sally gasped, and I had to agree. Sally was a rule follower and I'd have bet money she wouldn't hire someone if she knew they'd been in prison.

"Can we start at the beginning?" Trevor asked. "How did you meet your husband?"

"I joined a pen pal program for incarcerated people. I wrote to a couple of different inmates. At first, the letters between Peter and me were boring, talking about the weather and how the Cardinals were doing in that season. After a while, they became more personal. He told me about his life, about how he'd been jailed for assault with a deadly weapon, but he didn't go into a lot of details about the crime. He said he wanted to change, to be a different person when he got out. More time went by, more letters were sent, and I really fell for him. He had a way with words and made me feel very special."

"What did he say?" Trevor asked.

"Well, when I sent him pictures, he told me I was stunning. We spoke on the phone and said my voice soothed him. I began visiting him and he said my skin looked so soft and I was even prettier than in my pictures."

"A lot of flattery," Sally noted.

"Yes, but he also told me that I made him laugh and he loved listening to me talk, so it wasn't all about my looks."

"Go on," Trevor urged. "By the time he got out of prison, it seems like you two were pretty close."

"Yes. When he was released, I was there to pick him up... and one thing led to another and we were married."

"What prison was he in?" Trevor asked.

"Lewis. Out by Buckeye."

"And when did he get out?"

"About six months ago."

"Sally, how long had he been working for you?" Trevor asked.

"I'd have to look, but I'd say about five months."

"It sounds like he got out of prison and you two made your way up here, Mrs. Maven. Is that correct?"

"Yes."

"And how long were you two married?"

"Three months," she sighed.

A pang of pity hit my chest. They'd been newlyweds. How horrible for Whitney to lose her husband in such a short period of time.

"I'll be checking all this information,"

Trevor said. "Please make sure everything you say is accurate."

"I don't have anything to hide," Whitney said. "I haven't done anything wrong."

"Except you didn't meet us at the station as we requested," the second deputy snarled. "Why did you come here?"

"Because you told me my husband was murdered, and I couldn't believe it!" Whitney yelled. "Why wouldn't I come here?"

They sat in silence for a long moment. It probably would've been a good idea for them to wait to call the widow until they'd moved the body, but I wasn't in charge of the scene.

"Who did it?" Whitney asked. "Who killed Peter?"

"We don't know," Trevor replied. "We're following up on different leads."

"I was the last one to see him alive," Sally said. "We argued last night, but I didn't murder him."

"Mrs. Maven, weren't you concerned when your husband didn't return home last night after work?" Trevor asked.

"No."

"Why is that?"

A long pause ensued before she answered. "Because we were divorcing. We still lived together but I moved into the guest room."

Well, so much for my pity party. Apparently, there'd been trouble in the newlywed paradise.

"You didn't hear him come home most nights?"

"Sometimes I did, other times I didn't."

"Why are you divorcing?" Trevor asked.

"He's got a side piece, deputy. I don't know who she is, but he's admitted to cheating and I won't have any part of that. My husband needs to remain loyal to me and Peter hasn't been. Therefore, we're done."

"There wasn't any room for redemption?" Trevor asked.

"None."

"How did you find out he was cheating?"

"A text came through on his phone while he was in the shower," she replied. "It contained filthy, pornographic language on what this woman wanted to do to him. I guess you'd call it sexting."

"And you didn't see who it was from?"

"No. He'd given her some nickname. Sweet Something-or-another."

"Do we have his phone?" Trevor asked. "It wasn't on the body."

"If he doesn't have it, then it may be in his locker in back," Sally said. "I can go check if you like."

"We'll go in a minute," Trevor replied. "Stay right here for now, please."

"Will do, Deputy," Sally said.

I imagined Trevor scrawling furiously in his notebook, taking down all the details of his conversation with Whitney.

"Where were you last night, Mrs. Maven?" he asked.

"Home."

"By yourself?"

"Yes."

"Did you talk to anyone? See anyone? Go anywhere?"

"I'm sorry, but I didn't. I tried to call my sister to see if I could go visit her, but there wasn't any answer."

"Did you leave a message?"

"No."

"Why did you want to visit your sister?" he asked.

"Because I need to get out of town and away from... Well, I guess I don't have to worry about it anymore."

"You wanted to get away from your husband?" Trevor hedged.

"Yes. I haven't talked to my sister in a few weeks, but I thought maybe she'd take me in."

"Where does she live?"

"Colorado."

"And you two were close?" Trevor urged.

"We... we used to be. I don't see what my relationship with my sister has to do with anything."

"Gina, when are they going to be done talking?" Daisy asked. "I'm getting tired of sitting here under this table."

She wasn't the only one. However, I couldn't just announce myself at a murder scene then take my leave. I'd probably be thrown in jail for interfering with an investigation. She lay down next to me, sighed, and I hoped no one heard her doing so.

"You seemed quite upset for someone who's getting divorced," the other deputy said.

"Yes, I was divorcing him, but that doesn't mean I don't care. I didn't... I didn't want him dead."

"Can we go back to the fake name?" Sally asked. "Mario... or Peter, was a great cook. Why not use his real name?"

"He figured background checks would be done no matter where he applied, so he wanted a clean slate. Peter Smith became chef Mario Maven."

"Where did he learn to cook?" Sally asked.

"Prison."

"Oh, my," Sally whispered.

"See, he knew that would be the reaction

when an employer realized he or she was hiring a felon," Whitney said. "So, he invented Mario Maven. He wanted a flashy name, one that could never be misconstrued as Peter Smith. Had papers done and made up a resume."

"You didn't check on any prior jobs?" Trevor asked.

"No," Sally replied. "He was nice, polite, and made me a meal that knocked my socks off. I hired him on the spot."

"Who did he assault?" Trevor asked. "Do you know the name of the person?"

"No," Whitney sighed. "I never wanted to know the details of his prior life before he met me and he didn't give me a lot of them. He told me he was put away for assault, but that was it."

"That'll be in the arrest record," the second deputy said.

The room went quiet for a very long time. Daisy had fallen asleep next to me and snored softly. I almost wondered if everyone had left and I hadn't realized it.

"May I leave now?" Whitney asked, her voice cracking. "I want to go home."

"Yeah, go ahead," Trevor replied. "Please don't leave town. We'll need to talk to you later."

I glanced around the table leg and watched

her walk out. When the door shut, the second deputy said, "We should get her phone records and check out her statement about trying to contact her sister. We can also see if her cell phone pings close to the restaurant at any time last night."

"We will. Let's make sure to—"

The front door opened again and two EMTs wheeled in a gurney. A little friendly banter ensued between the deputies and emergency personnel, then the body was loaded onto the gurney and rolled out.

"Why don't you head back to the station and get started on Whitney's records?" Trevor instructed. "I'll stay here with Sally and go over the scene one more time, then collect Mario's phone. Or Peter. Whatever. I'll meet you back there shortly."

"Sounds good," the other officer said. "I'll see you in a bit."

After he exited, Sally said, "Should we head into the back and grab that phone?"

"Yes. You said he had a locker there?"

"Every employee does," she replied.

Their voices faded and I stretched out my legs. I assumed Sally would be escorted from the building after Trevor had collected the phone. They most likely wouldn't allow her to clean up until after they had completed the investigation and gathered all the evidence. It could be hours, it could be days. After everyone left, I'd take a closer look around, then Daisy and I would sneak out the back and head down to the Riverwalk.

At least it didn't appear Trevor believed Sally had anything to do with the killing. Maybe it was all Mallory, which wouldn't surprise me. I wished someone would run against her and our community could be done with her incompetence.

"Thanks for all your help, Sally," Trevor said, his voice sounding closer again. They must have come back into the main restaurant. "I'm sorry about Mallory being so harsh with you earlier."

"I didn't do this, Trevor," she said. "And I'll do whatever is necessary to find out who killed him."

"Thanks. This phone should be helpful, and we'll try to get the investigation wrapped up as soon as possible so you can clean up in here. But for the time being, I think the best thing would be for Gina to show herself and quit scurrying around the floor like a darn cockroach."

CHAPTER 3

Daisy opened her eyes and perked her ears. "Did I hear that right?"

"Yes," I whispered. "We've been busted."

She giggled as she stood and stretched. "That's pretty funny he let you sit here this whole time." She took off then, leaving me struggling to crawl out and stand.

"Did you see what a good girl I was, Trevor? Did you see how quiet I was? I was sooo good!" Daisy yelled.

"Hi, Daisy." Trevor sighed. "If you keep hanging around Gina, you're going to find yourself in trouble."

I stood and found him petting my traitorous dog.

"I'm a good girl, Trevor!" she said. "I won't let her get me in trouble!"

I smiled and wondered if Trevor realized he was having a conversation with her.

After a moment of stroking the dog's head, he glanced up at me. "What the heck, Gina?"

"How did you know I was here?" I asked.

He hitched his thumb over his shoulder. "I saw you come in through the reflection on the glass."

Oh. *I hadn't noticed that.*

"How the other deputy, Harry, didn't see you, I'll never understand," Trevor continued, shaking his head. "But then again, this was his first murder and he's pretty shaken. Poor guy just started a week ago."

"That's too bad," I said. "Trial by fire, I guess. He sounded confident while interviewing Whitney."

Or maybe it had all been an act. Fake it until you make it had been my motto for a number of years. I could only assume I wasn't the only one who followed the adage.

Trevor gripped the end of the leash so tight, his fingers turned white as he stared at the ceiling for a moment. It seemed I was precariously close to his last nerve. "Sit down, please," he said, pointing to the table. "And hold on to Daisy so she doesn't contaminate the scene."

I hurried over to the table and took her leash from him, then sat where Whitney had been. Sally came over to me and gave me a quick embrace, joining me at the table.

"What are you doing here?" Trevor asked.

"I noticed the police cars out front while we were on our walk and thought I'd stop by," I said.

"Pants on fire, liar!" Daisy called from beneath the table.

Ignoring her, I continued. "When I realized there was an ongoing investigation into a murder, I was shaken up and decided to hide."

"Oh, my gosh." Daisy snorted. "You are the worst liar ever."

Trevor rolled his eyes. "I don't think I believe you."

"I called her," Sally interjected. "Okay? Mallory scared me to death with her threats, so I called Gina."

"What in the world can Gina do for you?" he asked.

"She found out who killed Phoebe." She shrugged. "So, I figured she can figure out who killed Mario... or Peter. Whatever his name was."

"That's what the police do, Sally," he replied gently.

"Not very efficiently," I muttered. Trevor shot me a glare. "Look," I said. "I'm here. Maybe I can help."

"Me, too!" Daisy yelled. "My super-sniffer can find the bad guy!"

How in the world would I be able to let her go so she could smell the crime scene? Especially since Trevor had been adamant that I keep her leashed up and away from it? I couldn't. I was already pushing the limits with him just by being in the restaurant. One wrong move and he'd become furious, then kick me out of On The River, as well as the investigation. For Sally's sake, I had to mind my manners... and my dog.

He sighed and rubbed his forehead with his thumb. "You're giving me a headache."

"That's not very nice," I retorted. "Sally called and needed my help, so here I am. I can find out who killed the chef with or without you, Trevor." I turned to Sally. "You said you fought with Mario last night. Has anyone asked what you were arguing about?"

"Hey!" Trevor exclaimed. "This is my investigation!"

"I'm asking my friend a question," I shot back. "You can sit there and listen or you can leave."

So much for minding my manners.

Trevor muttered a curse, then turned his attention to Sally.

She cleared her throat. "There were a

couple of things. First, I got a phone call from a customer that they'd become sick after eating here. I was mortified."

"What did they eat?" I asked, hoping it wasn't my beloved breakfast burritos. I'd just picked up three of them yesterday and I'd hate to throw them out.

"A BLT with avocado," she said, pushing her glasses up her nose.

Thank goodness. "Was the avocado bad?" I asked.

She shook her head. "I discovered that the mayonnaise was out of date," she replied. "It was the only thing that could make someone sick. Everything else was made fresh, including the bread. The produce was delivered yesterday morning and I washed it myself."

"I'm sorry to hear that, Sally," Trevor said. "But why argue with him about it? Wasn't it an oversight on his part?"

"That's possible," she replied. Her stare had moved to where Mario had been killed. "I was very angry because I pride myself on running a clean restaurant where people get organic, healthy food. My online reviews are stellar, and I've passed all my health department inspections with perfect grades for ten years. And then someone got sick? Because Mario had been lazy and allowed the mayonnaise to go out of date?" She sighed and shook her head. "It's my reputation on the line, Deputy, not his."

Frankly, I had to agree with Trevor. It seemed a bit overkill to have a big argument over one sick customer. "Sally, was there something else that happened?"

Tears pooled in her eyes, then tracked down her cheeks. For a long moment, she continued to stare at where Mario had died. Finally, she spoke. "I'm afraid to say anything. I don't want to get into any more trouble."

As tension filled the air, I wondered what else Sally knew. She was a rule follower to the point where I imagined she had conflicted feelings about a rolling stop at an empty intersection.

"You won't get in trouble," I said, laying my hand over hers. When Trevor remained quiet, I glared at him. "Right, Deputy? She doesn't have to worry about sharing other bits of information that may be important in solving Mario's murder."

"Not unless she broke the law."

I rolled my eyes. "Do you want to solve this case or bust an innocent woman? Be better than your boss, Trevor. For the love of everything holy, please be better than that trainwreck."

Sally smiled while Trevor narrowed his gaze and Daisy giggled under the table.

"If she hasn't done anything illegal, she won't get in trouble," Trevor said through clenched teeth.

"Did you do something to break the law?" I asked Sally.

She shook her head.

"Well then, tell us what else you know," I urged.

After taking a deep breath, she shut her eyes. "You're right. It wasn't just the mayonnaise. One of the servers also saw him dealing drugs out of the kitchen back door. That's what she thought, anyway."

"Can you be more specific in describing what she saw?" Trevor asked.

"She said a man came here on a motorcycle. He knocked on the back door. Mario must not have realized she was in the pantry area, because he talked freely with the man after he was handed a package."

"What were they talking about?" I asked.

"Money. The man said Mario owed him for the package. Mario told him he needed to sell some of it first, then he'd give him the payment."

"Who was this server and how did she know the man arrived on a motorcycle if the back door was closed?" Trevor asked, his pen poised above his open notebook.

"She heard him drive up," Sally replied. "The bike was loud. When he opened the door, she saw it."

"What's her name?" Trevor asked, scribbling furiously.

"Ginny Winn."

I knew Ginny. She often came in to get her nails done at my salon, File It Away. In her late twenties, she'd been divorced twice and had three kids. I admired her ability to work full-time and be a single parent to three of the nicest kids I'd ever met.

"Did she confront Mario?" I asked.

Sally shook her head. "Ginny waited until the motorcycle guy left, then Mario hid the drugs behind some pans. When he turned away from her, she hurried out of the kitchen. A couple of hours went by until she told me what she'd witnessed. We were in the middle of dinner service, so I waited until we were closed to confront Mario."

"Did you locate the drugs?" Trevor asked.

Sally shook her head. "I pulled out all the pots and pans and the package wasn't there. Mario told me I was out of my mind, that he wasn't dealing drugs."

"Did your argument become physical?" Trevor asked.

"No. We did a lot of yelling, but there wasn't a physical altercation."

Trevor turned toward the door leading to the kitchen. "Let's go in there and you can show me everything."

I stood to follow but Trevor shook his head. "I need the dog to stay out of the murder scene."

"She will," I said. "I'll tie her to the leg of the table." I bent over and turned the leash into a very loose knot, one she should be able to dislodge with one tug. Hopefully she'd go sniff around and maybe, if we were lucky, she'd pick up on the murderer's scent.

I trailed them into the kitchen. When Trevor shot me a glare, I smiled. Eventually, he'd want my help on this case... if I didn't solve it first.

As Sally pointed at the back door and the metal table where the pots and pans were stored, I glanced around, barely hearing her repeating her story. A block of knives stood next to another table, and I walked over to them. One was missing.

"Is this where the murder weapon was?" I asked.

Sally nodded. "Whoever stabbed him used my favorite knife."

"Don't touch that, Gina," Trevor warned. "We were waiting for the body to be picked up before we dust for prints. It hasn't been done yet."

Trevor kneeled before the table where the pots and pans were kept. With his pen, he pushed a few aside. "This is where Ginny said the drugs were hidden?"

"Yes. I've been through all of them and there's nothing there."

"Maybe he sold all of it," I suggested. "Was there any money on him?"

Trevor shook his head. "Not a dollar."

"So maybe this was a robbery," I said. "Motorcycle guy arrives after Sally leaves, talks to Mario about collecting the money, they get into a scuffle, Mario gets stabbed and motorcycle man takes the drugs. Or the money, if Mario had sold them."

"It's a possibility," Trevor said. "Did Ginny get a look at the motorcycle guy?"

I walked into the pantry area. From the entry, the back door was in my line of sight. "My guess is yes," I said. "Even if she had this door closed a bit, she'd be able to see from this angle."

"She didn't know him, but she did have a description," Sally said.

"Was he wearing a helmet?" I asked.

"Not that I know of," Sally replied. "If so, he removed it before he talked with Mario."

Trevor stood and pulled out his notebook from his back pocket. "Go ahead. Tell me what he looked like."

"Big guy. He wore a biker cut, but she couldn't see the name. Beard with a handlebar mustache."

I groaned and crossed my arms over my chest.

"What's wrong?" Sally asked.

"I think I know him," I replied.

"Are you thinking what I'm thinking?" Trevor asked.

"Yes. I believe I am."

Trevor sighed and glanced around the restaurant. "I'll see you back at your house later today, Gina. I'll give you a call before I come over."

"I'll be ready."

CHAPTER 4

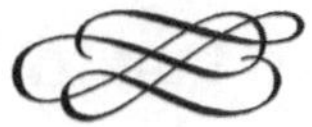

When Daisy and I were out the door, I asked, "Did you sniff around where the body was?"

"No. Was I supposed to?"

I glanced down at my little brown and white friend, shaking my head. "Are you kidding me? I left you with the perfect opportunity!"

"You left me tied to the table and it was time for a nap!"

"Daisy, I barely looped the leash at all. You could've easily pulled away. What happened to your super sniffer?"

She trotted along next to me for a moment. "I guess I wasn't a very good sleuth. I'm sorry, Gina."

"I think I better call my brother," I muttered.

"Why? What's Vic doing? Do you think he killed that man?"

"No, I don't. But he knows Handlebar and we obviously need to talk to him. I think a conversation with him will go a lot smoother with Vic there."

"Who's Handlebar?" Daisy asked.

Hailing from Sedona, Handlebar was a member of the motorcycle club there and he perfectly fit the description Sally had given. I'd heard around town he dabbled in the drug trade, as did my brother. They knew each other. Trevor and I going in and accusing Handlebar of killing Mario would only be trouble... unless Vic was present. He had a way about him that calmed others—namely, his fists.

"A guy Vic knows," I said, not bothering to explain it all to her.

We hurried home and Daisy stopped in the driveway.

"Um... Gina? Who's that?"

A Golden retriever sat on my porch, his tail wagging. "I have no idea."

"Is he mean?"

"I don't think they make Goldens mean, Daisy. I've never met one, anyway."

Still, I approached with caution. I estimated the big hunk of blond fluff to weigh about eighty to ninety pounds. He eyed me with warm eyes, his tail swishing back and forth. To my horror, he was tied to my porch.

"What the heck?" I whispered. As I stuck my hand out, he sniffed my fingers, then licked them. "What's your name, buddy?"

"Let's call him Buddy!" Daisy said. "That's a good name!"

As I stroked his head, I glanced up and down my street. Why would someone leave their Golden tied to my porch? A sinking feeling settled in the pit of my stomach. I knew the answer.

Because I was the local dog rescuer.

He had been well-fed and recently brushed, so he wasn't my usual rescue. Oftentimes, dogs arrived at my house in need of a bath and a few good meals.

Daisy stood behind me but sniffed around my feet. My new friend danced and whined as he eyed her.

I took one more look around the neighborhood. Not a soul. I untied him and sighed. "It looks like we've got a new roommate, Daisy."

The Golden barked and wagged his tail as I opened the door, then he ran inside, forcefully pulling the leash out of my hand. "And someone needs some manners," I muttered.

Daisy trailed after him to the living room. I found him sitting on the couch, already making himself at home.

"That's kind of rude," Daisy complained. "I at least waited for an invitation before getting on the couch."

"I know." I grabbed his collar and pulled him down while telling him *off* in my most threatening voice.

He growled and rolled over on his back, then sprang up and ran from the room down the hall.

What was with this canine? Poor manners? Bad upbringing? Or was he just a jerk?

I followed and found him on my son's bed.

"Get down," I ordered. "No dogs in this room."

He simply stared at me.

"Daisy!" I yelled. "Come in here and talk to this dog. Tell him there are rules to be followed in this house." It was so helpful having a dog that not only spoke to her own kind, but to me as well. I was able to understand the new dogs who came into my home much better with her assistance.

He wagged his tail as Daisy entered. After sitting at my feet, she stared at the Golden. The room went quiet for a moment as his ears perked while he watched her.

Banshee, my last rescue who sat by her food bowl all day, had finally been adopted by an older couple who just wanted some company. I was glad she wasn't with me any longer because I had the distinct feeling she wouldn't like this pushy beast.

"He said he doesn't like rules," Daisy muttered.

"What's his name?" I asked.

"Sir Zeus Belvedere."

I rolled my eyes. Who gave their pets such ridiculous monikers? "Are you kidding me?"

"I wish I was. He thinks he's better than the best pepperoni treat with peanut butter on top, and he doesn't make any sense."

I took that to mean the dog was full of himself and not a snack. "Ask him who his owners are."

She sighed and glanced at him, then said, "He's not going to tell you who they are, and I quote, 'neener, neener, neener.'"

"Get off the bed," I growled. He complied, then ran out into the hall.

As I trailed after him, I knew even if I had his owners' names, I wouldn't call. They didn't want him, and frankly, I was beginning to understand why. Trying to return a dog to somewhere he wasn't wanted went against every fiber of my being. They'd obviously tied him to my porch. This dog wasn't lost, but had been surrendered.

I found him in the kitchen with his front paws on the counter, chewing on my roll of paper towels.

"Enough!" I yelled as I grabbed his collar and pulled him off, then dragged him to the backdoor and threw him outside.

He barked once, then began sniffing around the yard. I leaned up against the door and took a few deep breaths.

"No manners at all," Daisy said, sitting in the middle of the kitchen as if she were the perfect princess. "I don't know what you're going to do about that, Gina, but I have to admit, he scares me a bit."

"He's not going to hurt you," I muttered. Then again he might, just not on purpose. "This is really the last thing I need right now."

"I know," Daisy replied. "I hope you get it worked out."

She stood and trotted down the hall. "Where are you going?" I called.

"To take a nap! Good luck, Gina!"

"Some help you are," I whispered.

What should I do first?

I glanced out the window and found Sir Zeus Belvedere rolling around in the grass, appearing to be the happy, gentle Golden retriever I imagined him to be. "Looks can be deceiving," I said to my empty kitchen.

With a murderer on the loose and me barging my way into the investigation, it would be a good idea to find another rescuer to take in Sir Zeus Belvedere. He needed a lot of work and training, and I simply didn't have the time. I pulled out my phone as he began to dig by the fence. He'd never get out since I had block walls. I'd always kept my yard simple because I did have dogs in and out all the time, and a lot of them had bad behaviors. Zeus could dig all he wanted, but eventually, he'd have to learn that wasn't acceptable conduct.

I phoned two other rescuers I knew. Both were full, which saddened and angered me. There were so many unwanted pups in the world, yet people kept breeding and not neutering.

After three other failed attempts to pawn the unruly Golden off on someone else, I realized he was going to be my responsibility.

I glanced out the window again. Big brown eyes stared up at me from the golden face, his tail slowly wagging. Sir Zeus Belvedere looked so harmless and loving. He'd just been dumped at a stranger's house, so I had to have patience with him.

"Come on in," I said, opening the door. As

he stood at my feet, I reached down and scratched under his chin. He quickly wrapped his jaws around my wrist, and for a brief second, fear caught in my throat. Then, when he didn't bite, I realized he was simply trying to play.

"Okay, big guy," I whispered, stroking his head. "We aren't going to play like that. I'll get you a tennis ball or something."

I gently pulled my wrist away and gave him a quick pat. Realizing I hadn't eaten yet, I grabbed a container of yogurt from the refrigerator, set it down on the counter, then turned to my phone to call my brother.

"Hey, Vic," I greeted him when he answered. "Are you free this afternoon?"

"What's up, Gina?"

"Well, I need you to come over. There was a murder at On The River, and I've kind of gotten myself involved."

"Why would you do that?" he asked.

"Because Sally needed me to," I replied. "Remember when you were accused of murder and begged me for help? It's kind of the same thing."

"Oh, man, that's too bad. What happened?"

I explained about Mario, aka, Peter being found lying across a table with a knife sticking out of his chest, and Handlebar possibly being involved as he'd been seen at the restaurant.

"So can you stop by?" I asked. "Trevor will be here."

"What does he want with me?" Vic asked. "I didn't have anything to do with it."

"I know, but Handlebar may be tangled up in this. I told Trevor you knew him, and maybe you can talk to him about the murder."

"Handlebar and I haven't seen each other in ages," Vic argued. "I'm out of that world, Gina."

With a sigh I shut my eyes and rubbed my thumb between my eyebrows as I leaned against the fridge. "That's great, Vic. I'm glad you cleaned up your life, but Handlebar hasn't. He's bad news, and we need to talk to him. He's not going to spill any secrets to me and a cop, but he may speak with you."

A long stretch of silence ensued then a horse whinnied in the background. "Hold on, big fella," Vic said soothingly. "Let me hang up and we'll get back to business."

My phone buzzed in my hand and I glanced at the messages. Trevor had texted.

BE THERE IN TWO HOURS.

. . .

"Can you be here in a couple of hours?" I asked.

"I guess so," Vic said. "But I'm not sure why I need to stick my toe into the murky waters I've left behind."

"Aren't you philosophical," I snorted. "Just be here in two hours. You're doing this because you owe me. I made sure you didn't go to jail for murdering your ex-girlfriend."

"And I thought we were even because I saved your life when you were tied up in a barn."

Well, maybe we were even.

"Just get over here," I sighed, then hung up.

I really liked the idea of Handlebar being the killer. Ginny had seen him delivering the drugs, and Mario had owed him money. For all I knew, the biker had been responsible for a dozen deaths. I only hoped Vic would be able to tease information out of him.

Turning to grab my yogurt, I didn't find it where I'd left it on the counter. Had I placed it somewhere else?

I glanced around the kitchen. My roll of paper towels, as well as the wooden holder they had been on, were also gone.

"Uh oh," I whispered. I'd forgotten about my new charge while talking to Vic.

I hurried into the living room and found Zeus on the couch lying on his back. Between his front paws he held the roll of paper towels. Bits and pieces had scattered around him and onto the floor where the empty yogurt cup and my now broken paper towel holder also lay. With a light growl, he ripped some of the paper off, chewed on it for a moment, then allowed it to fall out of his mouth.

As I watched him, I tried to remain calm. I had to remember he was most likely scared and upset being in a new place, but I also realized that if I didn't get this dog under control, he could very well destroy my house.

Somehow, I had to find the time to train the dog, find him a new home, *and* catch a killer.

CHAPTER 5

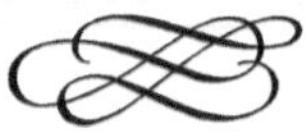

I ENDED up giving Sir Zeus Belvedere a couple of CBD chews, and by the time Vic and Trevor arrived, he relaxed on the couch, barely able to keep his eyes open.

"Who's the new tenant?" Vic asked.

"Someone left him on my porch," I replied.

"Aren't Golden retrievers usually a little more rambunctious?"

"Trust me, he is," I said, crossing my arms over my chest as I stared at the big blond fluff-ball. "I had to give him something to mellow him out. He's a bit of a trouble causer."

"That's probably why he was surrendered."

"I'm sure," I said. "Speaking of rescues, how's Sing?"

Sing was the chow that had chosen Vic as his own while my brother had hidden out at my house and I attempted to find who'd killed his ex-girlfriend.

"He's great," Vic said. "He loves watching me work with the horses, and also likes to nap in piles of hay in the barn. I'm constantly finding straw on the couch or in my bed."

"I'm glad he's worked out so well," I said, smiling. It truly warmed my heart when a dog I'd rescued found their forever home.

"Where's Daisy?" Vic asked.

"I'm right here, Vic!" she yelled as she ran down the hall, then sat at his feet, her tail going so fast it was nothing but a brown and white blur. "I'm right here! Pet me, Vic! Pet me!"

As Vic bent over and ran his hand over Daisy's head, Trevor arrived. Daisy said hello to him, then we had basically the same conversation about Zeus that I'd had with Vic.

Both men greeted him as he wagged his tail lazily. Later, I'd do some work with him and see if he'd had any training and what knowledge he needed to acquire so I could get him adopted. A Golden retriever would be in high demand, but he had to be able to mind his manners and live within the rules set for him.

Vic, Trevor, and I sat down at the kitchen table. I'd made a pot of coffee, and both sipped their afternoon fuel greedily.

Trevor ran a hand through his blond hair

and sighed, shutting his eyes for a moment while Daisy curled up on my feet.

"It must've been one heck of an afternoon," Vic said. "You okay there, copper?"

Trevor opened his eyes. "Yeah, I'm good. I've got a long investigation in front of me, though."

"You still want me there to talk to Handlebar?" Vic asked.

"I do, but I have a few other suspects I need to check out as well."

"Who?" I asked, pushing my glasses up my nose. When I'd left, there'd been two suspects: Sally and Handlebar. Sally hadn't done it, so I was focused on Handlebar. Now there were more?

"Well, we've got the two you know about," Trevor said. "But there's a couple more people who have come across my radar."

"How did that happen?" I asked.

"Well, first and foremost, we got into Mario's phone. I'm just going to stick with Mario, even though his real name is Peter, if that's okay."

"It's fine with me," I said. "Mario has a bit of flare to it. Much more exciting than being named Peter."

"Good," Trevor said. "After I got into

Mario's phone, it became apparent that Whitney isn't as innocent as she appeared."

"Who's Whitney?" Vic asked.

"Mario Maven's wife who said she was about to become the ex-wife," I said. "What did you find in his phone?"

"She threatened to kill him the night he was murdered," Trevor said. "They were texting back and forth about money, and she said she'd kill him if he didn't give her the profits from the sale of their house."

"I thought divorce meant you split everything fifty-fifty," I said. When I'd gone through divorce all those years ago, we hadn't had anything monetary to fight over, so he'd gone his way and I'd gone mine. He also hadn't had much interest in being a father, so I'd won there as well.

"That's the way it's supposed to be, but she was threatening him. She also didn't have an alibi, so we have to consider her a suspect."

Based on what I'd heard, I couldn't imagine Whitney hurting anyone, but she had found out her husband was cheating. My husband had also been a serial cheater and I'd been furious. But would I have killed him? Honestly, the cheating was the least of his sins, so if I had done him in, it would've been for something else, like him laying hands on me. "Who was the second woman?" I asked. "Did you get her name?"

"Second woman?" Vic asked, arching his eyebrows. "This is getting good."

"Yes, a second woman named Tara Greene, otherwise known as *Sweet n' Sassy Lady* on Mario's phone."

Vic and I exchanged glances. We'd both lived in Heywood our whole lives, but I didn't recognize the name. However, being the lady's man he was, I had a feeling Vic may have.

"I don't know her," he said, holding up his hands.

"She lives in Sedona," Trevor replied. "Still doesn't ring any bells?"

Vic shook his head. I didn't bother to mention that he could've known her intimately and not be familiar with her name. It wouldn't be the first time.

"Why is she a suspect?" I asked.

"She's not, but I need to speak with her," Trevor said. "There seemed to be a little tension in their correspondence in between the juicy stuff."

"What kind of tension?" I asked.

"She really, really wanted him to leave Whitney and move to Sedona to be with her, but Mario wanted to stick it out until the divorce was final. She wasn't happy about that."

"I find it odd that Whitney and Mario were okay sharing the same house," I said. "I would think they'd want to at least get different roofs over their heads."

"Maybe they couldn't afford it until the house sold," Vic proposed.

"But Mario was offered a new place to stay in Sedona," I said. "Why didn't he take it?"

Both men exchanged glances, then shrugged.

"Would either of you want to continue to live with your wife who wanted to divorce you?" I asked.

"Nope," both answered in unison.

"So why was he sticking around?"

"Maybe the drug trade out of the back door of Sally's restaurant was going particularly well," Trevor suggested.

"Or maybe he wanted to make sure Whitney didn't trash the house," Vic chimed in.

"Why would she do that?" I asked. "She'd get something out of the sale. If the house was trashed, then there'd be nothing for either of them."

"I don't know," Vic said. "I'm just throwing out ideas."

We sat in silence as I pondered why Mario would stay with Whitney in the same house when he had an invitation to move elsewhere. What was keeping him in Heywood? Did he hope he and Whitney would get back together? Or was it the money he was making illegally at On The River? Or maybe Sally paid him particularly well and he didn't want to lose that. He had been in prison and lied to get the job. Maybe he was afraid another employer would dig deeper into his background than Sally had and find his secret.

Trevor cleared his throat. "I also looked into Mario's arrest record and found some interesting tidbits."

"Like what?" Vic asked.

"Mario was put in prison for almost killing a rival drug dealer. That man could've been looking to get revenge."

"That's a big jump," I said. "Do we even know where he lives?"

Trevor nodded. "Yep. Billy Hoffman, the guy who Mario almost killed, lives up the freeway past Flagstaff."

"When did he move into the area?" I asked. "That's quite the coincidence."

"Yes. He moved in about three months ago."

Since Mario had been living in Heywood for five to six months, it definitely seemed as if

Billy was following him... and could possibly want to kill him as an act of revenge.

"Who else is on your list?" Vic asked. "This is better than the gossip at the bar."

"Well, I did a little digging into Mario's prison stint. He was approached by authorities who stated that Mario could get out early if he helped them bust open the drug ring within the prison."

"Did he bite?" Vic asked.

"Who bit who?" Daisy said from beneath the table. "Is someone biting someone else?"

I reached down and stroked her head instead of answering. Explaining that I was speaking to my talking dog wasn't high on my list of things to do, especially since it would sound like I'd lost my mind.

"He did," Trevor said, rocking back in his chair so far, the two front legs lifted from the floor. If he fell over, I wouldn't try to hide my amusement. "He received a reduced sentence for turning in a guy who goes by the name of Hornet."

"What's his real name?" I asked.

"Harry Dingle."

Vic burst out laughing. "I'd go by a different name, too."

I snickered and shook my head. Twelve-year-old-boy humor still made me giggle.

"Harry Dingle got extra time in prison because of what Mario did, and Mario got out a little earlier," Trevor continued. "When I spoke to the prison, Harry, or Hornet, was not happy. They had to move him to a different wing of the big house."

Heavy breathing followed by the clip clap of nails against the floor had all of us turning our heads. Zeus had entered the kitchen. He pushed past my leg to go under the table, then growled at Daisy.

"Hey!" I yelled, leaning over to scold him. "You're a guest in this house. You don't growl at my dog."

"Yeah, you big turd!" Daisy yelled. "I'll eat a pepperoni treat and let the worst smell you've ever experienced loose right in your face!"

Zeus lay down almost on top of her, forcing her to move.

"You are such a jerk," she hissed before trotting out of the kitchen and down the hall. Zeus moved into her position on top of my feet. As he was far heavier than my little forty-pound mutt, my feet would be asleep soon.

"What does Hornet have to do with anything?" I asked, attempting to ignore Zeus and get back to trying to figure out who'd killed Mario.

"Well, Hornet got out of jail about a month ago," Trevor explained.

"Is he violent?" Vic asked.

Trevor nodded. "He was also in for assault. According to his arrest record, he put a guy in the hospital with a concussion, a broken arm, and a few broken ribs and some missing teeth. If he hadn't been interrupted, he probably would've killed him."

"So he got out of prison last week," Vic said. "Did they say where he was heading?"

"Michigan."

"Well, that prospect is dead," I said.

"So what's your gameplan?" Vic asked. "It sounds like you've got a lot of bad dudes to question."

"I agree," Trevor sighed.

"Let's start with Handlebar," I suggested. "He knows Vic, and he may even be able to provide us with some information about the other guys. It seems like they're all cut from the same cloth, and drug dealers tend to keep tabs on other dealers."

Trevor arched an eyebrow.

"Well, so I've heard," I amended. "That's what happens on television, anyway."

And watching my brother dabble in that world had also given me a little knowledge on how things worked. His "retirement" from that lifestyle after Phoebe died had surprised me, but I was glad he was trying to live an honest life.

"She's got a good point," Vic said. "Let me call Handlebar and see when we can meet."

"Don't tell him he's a suspect in a murder," Trevor ordered. "And don't tell him you're bringing a cop with you. He may run scared."

"Or become violent," I said under my breath.

The last thing we needed was to tangle with a violent drug dealer.

CHAPTER 6

THE NEXT DAY, I tried to work with Zeus. He understood *sit*. He just didn't like doing it. He understood *stay*, but only for a brief moment, and then he came barreling at me and didn't stop, sending me to the ground wondering if my knee would work right once I was standing again.

"He's so stupid," Daisy said while watching him running around the yard. "He's got rocks for brains."

"Ask him what he needs," I said before getting up. Staring at the clouds in the sky above me I thought I saw a rabbit in one, and maybe a rain shower in the other. "It's obviously not approval," I continued. "He couldn't care less whether I'm impressed with him or not."

"Don't make me talk to him," Daisy whined as I staggered to my feet.

Zeus did another lap around the yard, then ran at me again. I realized he was trying to knock me over once more so I sidestepped him before he made contact.

"Alright," I said, turning toward the house. "Let's go inside."

I almost fell again when Zeus walked right in front of me, then began chewing on my sneaker. "No!" I yelled.

He didn't care.

After a moment, I grabbed him by the collar and yanked him away from my feet. I'd have liked to toss his unruly butt over the fence but instead, I cursed and hurried inside with Daisy right behind me.

I shut the door in Zeus's face.

"What are you going to do about him?" Daisy asked. "He's horrible."

"You could help me, you know," I replied, crossing my arms over my chest as I watched him jump up outside the window. "You could talk to him."

"Most of the time, he doesn't make any sense when I try to," she huffed. "It's like he can't put all the words in the right order."

Furrowing my brow, I turned to my talking

dog. 'He can't put all the words in the right order?"

"Yes. His brain has malfunctioned."

Zeus began to bark, then placed his paws against the window.

"So, he's big and his brain doesn't work."

"Pretty much."

"I'm not sure what to do with this dog," I murmured. "Maybe he needs more exercise." He'd slept in the laundry room last night after tearing apart the dog bed I had for him. Destruction seemed to be his middle name.

"Maybe he needs to get lost."

"Daisy, please don't talk like that," I scolded. "Somewhere, someone has a perfect home for him. We'll find him a match."

"I highly doubt it."

As I watched the Golden run around the yard again, I debated what to do with him. Handlebar had agreed to meet Trevor, Vic and me at Hold Your Horses, a bar just outside of Heywood.

"I better get going," I said.

"You will *not* leave me at home alone with that crazy beast," Daisy protested. "I don't care where you're going or how long I have to wait in the car."

"Daisy, I'm going to a bar. No dogs allowed."

Although it was the middle of the afternoon and I wasn't even sure if they'd be open to the public. With my friend, Rainy, being the bartender, she might allow Daisy in without a second thought.

"I don't care, Gina. I've never been more serious. I'm not staying with that big jerk."

"Fine," I grumbled. "Sit in the car all afternoon for all I care." With it being fall, I didn't have to worry about her dying in the heat. She'd be okay with the windows rolled down. I hurried into the bathroom and ran a brush through my blonde hair, then added a little blush and some mascara.

"Who are you getting all fancy for?" Daisy asked. Glancing in the mirror, I found her sitting in the doorway, her brown and white head tilted to the side.

"No one."

"I know it isn't me," she said. "I've seen you at your absolute ugliest, and I still like you."

I furrowed my brow. "My absolute ugliest? What does that mean?"

"Remember a couple months ago you had a bad cold and your eyes were swollen shut? Then your nose was red and puffy. You were so ugly, you scared me one morning when I woke up next to you."

It was at times like this that I wondered if my conversations with my dog were a figment of my imagination. This was something I would've said to someone, but not meant it in a cruel way—just stating a fact.

"Is it Trevor?' she asked. "I like Trevor. You should lick him."

"No, I don't put on makeup to impress men, and I'm certainly not going to lick him."

"You *should* try to impress him," Daisy said, her tail wagging slowly. "He's cute."

I shook my head and did a final check in the mirror. Was I trying to make Trevor swoon over me? Maybe a little. But I'd never in a gazillion years admit that to my talking dog, or anyone else, for that matter.

"Okay, are you ready to go?" I asked.

"Yes. Thank you for taking me and not leaving me home with the blond beast from the nether region."

I locked Zeus in the laundry room and heard him scratching the door as we left. If he'd broken it down by the time we arrived home, I wouldn't be surprised.

The drive out to Hold Your Horses was easy, especially with tourist traffic heading toward town.

I pulled into the dirt lot and parked next to Vic's pickup truck. Besides his vehicle and a motorcycle, which I assumed belonged to Handlebar, I was the only one there. Hold Your Horses hadn't opened yet.

"I guess Trevor isn't here," I sighed.

"That's okay," Daisy replied. "It gives you a chance to try to fluff your hair and check your makeup."

I glared at my dog through the rearview mirror. Fluffing my straight, fine blonde hair had never been an option. It simply didn't "fluff." And even if it did, I wouldn't do it for a stupid meeting in a dive bar. "I'm not trying to impress him."

"Whatever, Gina. Can we go inside?"

"Let me check and see if Rainy is here and gives me the okay." I rolled down the back window, then exited the car.

When I opened the door to the bar, the stench of stale cigarette smoke and beer slammed into me. After a second, my eyes adjusted and I found Vic and Handlebar sitting at the bar. Rainy waved from behind it. The silence was almost deafening. I tried to recall when I'd been inside this place without the music blaring, and nothing came to mind.

"Can I bring Daisy in?" I asked.

Rainy nodded, her gray curls bobbing around her face.

I opened the door and almost tripped over

Daisy who was sitting at the entrance. "You jumped out of the car?" I hissed. "How many times do I have to tell you that's dangerous?"

Ignoring me, she trotted inside, her nose to the ground. She complained about Zeus not listening, but she wasn't exactly obeying my commands, either.

With a sigh, I hurried over to the bar. Vic stood and hugged me while Handlebar glared at me. Shelves of booze stood behind Rainy, surrounding a yellowing mirror. I guessed the coloring was from years of cigarette smoke.

"Hey, Handlebar," I said, smiling. I refused to be intimidated by him, especially with my brother present. Vic would settle for nothing but respect from the biker.

"I'm not happy to be here," he growled.

"Are you ever happy to be anywhere?" I asked.

Vic chuckled. "Let's sit down at a table."

"Are you guys drinking, or can I go in back and finish up my accounting from last night?" Rainy asked.

"Whisky for me," Handlebar said.

"Make that two," Vic agreed.

I shook my head when my gaze met Rainy's. "Nothing for me, but thanks."

Vic led us over to a four top. After a moment, Rainy came over with the drinks. We sat in silence as the two men sipped their whisky. Searching the bar, I found Daisy in the far corner. She glanced up at me and wagged her tail, then continued her exploration. What she was looking for—if anything—I had no idea. Chances were good she was just doing dog things. The smells in the ancient building must be fascinating and abundant.

"I don't like you accusing me of murder, Gina," Handlebar said.

Not quite ready to say he was the killer, I replied, "I'm not."

"Then why am I here?" he asked.

"We know Mario was dealing drugs and you were his supplier," I replied, turning and hoping to find Trevor walking in sooner rather than later. I hated the idea of having the conversation twice.

"I wasn't there."

Shaking my head, I rolled my eyes. "Whatever, Handlebar. We have an eyewitness."

"No, you don't," he said. "They're wrong."

"The description she gave certainly sounds like you," Vic chimed in. "Big guy with a handlebar mustache wearing a biker club cut... you're the only guy I know with a mustache like that."

"It wasn't me."

I exchanged glances with Vic. Maybe we'd been wrong about Handlebar's involvement.

"Are you still dealing drugs?" Vic asked.

Handlebar took a long sip of his whisky. "I plead the fifth."

"Tell me you're still dealing drugs without telling me you're still dealing drugs," I snorted.

Just then, the front door opened and Trevor strolled in with his mouth in a hard, set line. He either meant business or he was having a horrible day.

No one said anything as he sat down, his focus solely on Handlebar.

"We can place you at On The River the night Mario Maven was killed," Trevor began as he flipped around the chair and straddled it. He glared at Handlebar for a long moment, then said, "Do you have anything you want to tell me about his death?" Apparently, there wouldn't be any small talk.

Handlebar furrowed his brow and slammed his fist against the table. "I got nothing to tell you, cop, except that I didn't have jack-all to do with his murder." He pointed to me and Vic. "You didn't tell me the dang cops would be here."

"I guess I forgot to mention it," Vic said innocently. "My bad, man. That was dumb of me."

"I ought to pound your face," Handlebar hissed.

"You can try, but I promise you, the outcome won't be in your favor," Vic retorted.

This wasn't going well. I didn't expect Handlebar to confess, but Trevor had come on too strong, the biker was angry at his presence, and the conversation was going to stop before it even started.

"Hang on a second," I said. "I'm sorry you didn't know the cops were going to be here, but Handlebar, what can you tell us about Mario?"

He stared at me a long moment, his jaw working.

"Listen, at this point, no one cares if you're dealing drugs," I continued. Whether it was true or not, I had no idea, and I didn't turn to Trevor for any input. If the idea was to find Mario's killer, drug-dealing seemed like child's play. We needed to know what Handlebar knew about the dead chef. "Let's say you *weren't* there that night, but can we at least agree that you and Mario know each other?"

"Yeah, we did."

Okay, at least we'd established a connection.

"What can you tell me about him?" I asked.

A long stretch of silence ensued. "Come on. Give us something to help us catch this killer."

"You help us, and I leave you alone," Trevor said. "Unless the video footage shows you murdering him."

Wait a minute. Video footage? I hadn't heard about that tidy piece of evidence. Where had Sally hidden the cameras?

As I attempted to keep my facial features neutral, a moment of doubt flickered across Handlebar's face while he pursed his lips.

"I didn't kill anyone," Handlebar repeated, crossing his arms over his barrel chest. "But I may have some information you'll like, as long as it keeps you off my butt and out of my business."

"That depends," Trevor said. "I don't care about the drugs now, but I may in the future. At the moment, I want Mario's killer."

"Mario was in prison with a guy named Harry Dingle," Handlebar said.

"We know. And Mr. Dingle goes by Hornet. That's not news," Trevor said. "Give me something new."

"Did you know Mario squealed on him and got him more prison time?" Handlebar asked.

Trevor nodded. "Yes, and we also know he's out now and headed to Michigan."

A smile spread across Handlebar's face. "And that's where you're wrong."

"What do you mean?" Trevor asked. "That's where he told the prison officials he would be reporting for probation."

"Harry Dingle, aka, Hornet was in Sedona last week at our bike club," Handlebar said. "After a few drinks, he was talking about getting revenge for Mario backstabbing him."

I couldn't hide my gasp. "What kind of revenge was he talking about?"

"Murder."

CHAPTER 7

TREVOR FOLLOWED me home from Hold Your Horses. My hands shook as I tried to insert the key into the front door. Hornet had claimed he wanted to murder Mario. It sounded like he may have followed through.

"Where's the Golden?" Trevor asked once we were inside.

"The laundry room," I replied. "He likes to destroy things and there's not a lot in there, so that's where I keep him when I'm out."

Trevor followed me to the door. After I opened it, Zeus bolted into the hallway and ran toward the living room. Daisy screamed, and as they flew past us, I realized the chase was on.

"You'll never catch me, you idiot!" she yelled while Trevor and I studied the destruction in the laundry room.

"Not much in there for him to get to, huh?" Trevor said, chuckling.

Zeus had pulled down the white laundry basket from the washing machine and ripped it apart. Bits and pieces of the plastic were scattered across the floor. He'd also lifted his leg against the dryer and destroyed a blue towel, which lay in strips among the basket bits across the tile.

"Oh, my word," I whispered, placing my hands on my hips.

The two dogs flew past us again, Daisy taunting him at the top of her lungs. "I'm too fast for you, dummy!"

When Zeus bumped into my legs and sent me into the laundry room crashing against the washer, Trevor said, "I'll get him outside."

While he wrangled the dogs out back, I retrieved the broom and dustpan, then pulled out some old towels to soak up the urine.

"Maybe he just needs more exercise," Trevor said once he'd returned and leaned over to grab the larger pieces of the laundry basket. "I'm going hiking tomorrow. Do you want to go?"

I shook my head. "I have appointments scheduled at File It Away."

"Can I take the dog and see if a hike helps his disposition?"

"Sure. I'd appreciate that."

"I promise not to lose him," Trevor said.

"Don't promise me that," I replied.

As our gazes met, we both smiled.

"Does the dog rescuer want me to get rid of her charge?" he asked.

I shook my head as guilt washed through me. "No. I shouldn't have said that. He's awful, but I can't have him lost in the hills. Make sure to bring him back to me. I'll figure out what to do with him."

Daisy screeched so loudly, I heard her despite me being inside. "Help! Help! Gina! Let me inside! Now!"

"I better let Daisy in," I said.

"How do you know she wants to come in?" Trevor asked, taking the broom from me.

"Just an idea," I muttered. No way was I admitting I could hear the dog speaking to me, even though Trevor had teased me about it a million times. Little did he know how right he'd been.

I hurried to the kitchen and opened the door. Daisy ran inside yelling, "Shut it! Shut it!"

As she skidded across the kitchen floor, I closed the door, leaving Zeus outside. He quickly turned his attention to the hole he was digging by the fence.

"Find someone to take that jerk!" she huffed. After taking a quick drink of water, she trotted down the hall to our bedroom while I returned to the laundry room.

"What a mess," Trevor said as he stuffed bits of towel into the garbage bag. "I don't know what you're going to do with that dog."

I took the broom from him. "Me neither."

Twenty minutes later, my laundry room was cleaned up and we moved to the kitchen.

"What did you think about our talk with Handlebar?" he asked while I poured us a couple of waters. We sat at the table.

"It sounds like Hornet is your guy," I replied. "I mean, Handlebar heard him say he wanted to kill Mario, and he lied to the police about where he was headed after being released."

"He's definitely someone I need to speak with," Trevor agreed. "But what did you think about Handlebar as the killer?"

"Well, he was there that night," I said, but then I remembered Trevor had mentioned cameras. "What did the camera footage show? I didn't even know Sally had any."

"She doesn't," he replied. "She claimed that she was old-fashioned and believed everyone deserved to be trusted, so she never installed any."

"So you lied to Handlebar?"

He shrugged. "Pretty much. I was hoping if he thought there were cameras, he'd just confess."

"Then you don't know Handlebar very well," I said. I took a sip of my water and set the glass down. "He lies about everything."

"Well, I tried."

"I was hopeful about those cameras," I said. "That's a big bummer they aren't real."

He nodded and twisted the glass between his fingers. "The place next door may have some footage I can use," Trevor said.

"Too Hot To Handle?" I asked.

"Yeah. I have a call in to the owner, Chris Raves. Hopefully, he'll get back to me today. I saw a camera by his door, but some store owners only have them for show, to use them as a deterrent. I hope that's not true with him."

"Well, maybe he'll have something that will help," I said.

"He's a good guy, so I'm sure he'll call back," Trevor said. "When I stopped by the store yesterday, there were so many people in there. His business is doing well."

Too Hot To Handle was the local hot sauce joint, and a huge draw for tourists. Chris grew all his own peppers and made sauces with names like Tearjerker, Devil's Juice and Hot

Mama. He dished out samples liberally for those brave enough to try his product. I personally loved his Hell on Earth over my eggs.

"I wish Handlebar had been a little more forthcoming regarding where we could find Hornet," I said.

"His reaction was to be expected," Trevor said. "He's no snitch."

And he'd made that quite clear with a string of colorful language.

"I'll have Sedona police go to the clubhouse and shake some people down. Maybe Hornet will even be there, and they can nab him for questioning."

"Wouldn't that be handy."

"Do you have a busy day tomorrow?" he asked. "Will you be working late?"

"Not too bad. I think I'll be done by three."

"Would you like to grab some dinner?"

The question caught me off guard. Was he asking me out on a date? Or just friends meeting for dinner?

I had no idea, so I shook my head, mainly because the idea of being on a date scared the heck out of me. "I-I can't leave the dogs here by themselves," I stuttered. "As you've witnessed, Zeus can't be trusted."

My rescues were always a good excuse for

me to cancel plans I didn't want to attend. Yes, I'd been thinking about getting back into the dating scene, especially with my son, Jacob, away at college, but I wasn't sure if I wanted to date a cop, or if I even wanted to date. It seemed safer to just say no and consider it further.

"Yeah, I forgot about that," he said, his face falling. I almost felt guilty for saying no. "Okay, I'll come get the dog about nine tomorrow. Does that work with your appointments?"

Appointments? Right. I had appointments at File It Away. I had become so flustered, I'd briefly forgotten. "Y-yes. The first one is at ten."

"Great. I should be back about 3:30, so the timing works out perfectly."

I nodded, then stood and walked him to the door. Had he been asking me out on a date, or was his intention merely two friends going to dinner? Embarrassment warmed my cheeks while I considered the question. I was too flustered to even question him about it.

"See you in the morning," he said, then left.

I shut the door and stared at it for a long while. Clarification on what his intentions were would be a good thing to have, but I was embarrassed I couldn't tell the difference between someone wanting to date me and a friend asking me to dinner.

After I'd kicked out my husband, my sole focus had been my son. I had no time for men, and now I was so out of practice, a dinner invitation had me flustered.

"You are pathetic," I said to the door.

"Yes, you are," Daisy said while trotting down the hallway toward me. "You could've gone to a steakhouse and brought me treats home, but instead, you're looking at the door."

She sat at my feet and stared up at me. "You should've thought about your dog before making such a rash decision."

I rolled my eyes and headed for the backyard. "Come with me," I called out. "I need to know exactly what Zeus is saying."

"But I don't want to be near him!" Daisy whined.

Once I got to the door, I turned and glared at her. "Get over here, or no jerky treats."

"You are so mean."

"It'll only take a minute." A bit of guilt washed through me. I hated threatening her.

"Fine. But if I do this, I get double jerky treats."

My guilt quickly turned to irritation. She always had the upper hand. I opened the door and stepped outside. Zeus jumped on me, placing his paws on my shoulders, then gave my face a good tongue-washing.

"Okay, thank you. Now get down," I said firmly, pushing him away. I looked at Daisy. "Ask him what I can do to make him mind. Does he need more exercise? Has he been fed well?" Maybe he had a vitamin deficiency?

She sat down and stared at him. After a moment, she looked at me. "Zeus says goober gotten goober and muffin turtles run."

"What? That doesn't make any sense, Daisy."

"Tell me about it. He's out of his mind."

The Golden spun around in a circle, then ran around the yard three times before finally collapsing and rolling onto his back. After a moment, he was up and at it again.

As I watched him, I wondered if it was possible for dogs to have ADD or ADHD? And if so, what did I do about it?

"I better call the vet," I said. I'd wanted to get Zeus checked out anyway.

"For me?" Daisy asked. "Please, not for me. I've been so good! And I feel fine! I don't need to go to the vet!"

"It's not for you." I leaned over and stroked her head. "It's for Zeus."

"Oh, okay," she said. "Maybe they'll give

him a bunch of shots while he's there. He deserves it."

Boy did he ever.

I had no idea how I was going to get this dog adopted without lying through my teeth about his demeanor.

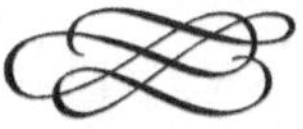

After Trevor took the dog the next morning, I got ready to head to the nail salon. Thankfully, our interaction hadn't been weird. He'd even brought me a coffee and croissant, then told a terrible joke.

"Where did the deer go to get his tail fixed?" he'd asked, his gaze twinkling with amusement.

"I have no idea."

"The re-tail shop."

He'd laughed so hard a tear trickled down his face. Despite rolling my eyes, I couldn't contain my giggles. But was it from the horrible joke, or Trevor's reaction to it?

When I arrived at the nail salon with Daisy in tow, I checked the scheduling app on my phone. To my surprise, Whitney Maven was there. She hadn't been last night, which was the last time I checked my calendar for the day.

"How weird is it to have your husband killed and then get your nails done?" I asked.

"Pretty weird," Daisy replied. "She doesn't seem that sad if she's worrying about her nails."

"Agreed." But it would be interesting to speak with her. I'd heard most of her story while hiding under the table at On The River, but she hadn't known I'd been there. Maybe she'd say something that didn't match up with what she'd told the cops.

I loved working at my nail salon, mainly because of the gossip that flowed through there. In the past, I'd gone on record claiming to hate gossip, but nothing could be further from the truth. Having a pulse on the community and knowing the dirt on everyone filled my heart with joy. Not that I ever did anything with the information I gathered—I just appreciated being in the know. At File It Away, I always discovered exactly what was going on in town, including at the highest political levels, as well as who was doing what with whom.

I was an excellent listener.

My first customer was Adrienne, the owner of our local wine shop, Never Quit Wining. Tall and lanky with flaming red hair, she strolled in as if she were on a catwalk, effortlessly placing one foot directly in front of the other while her hips gently swayed from side to side. She never realized she moved or looked like a super model.

"Hey, Adrienne," I called. "Take a seat."

I hurried over to her as she slipped off her shoes. After filling her foot bowl, she placed her feet in and sighed. "That feels so good."

"I bet," I said. "How's business?"

"Great," she sighed, closing her eyes. "I think we're going to have to find some help. I'm just exhausted."

"Isn't your customer base mainly tourists?" I asked.

"Yes."

"You know things will slow down in the winter when the snow hits, right?"

"Yes, but we're also working on an online store. Even then, I think we'll continue to be busy. And, it looks like we're going to pair with the ski resort. They'll be serving our bottles!"

Adrienne and her husband made their own wine. I'd had the pleasure of sampling more than a few bottles, and it was delicious. I found it much cleaner and more enjoyable than anything store bought. Adrienne had explained that was because they didn't use any sulphates and other garbage big wine manufacturers used.

"That's wonderful," I said, truly impressed. I loved watching people succeed. They'd been open just over a year and were making huge gains.

Just as I started scrubbing her feet, the front door chimed again. Daisy barked and ran across the store to the door where my friend, Annabelle, entered. She wasn't on the schedule, so it must be a social call. I hadn't seen her in a few days, and I appreciated her stopping by.

"Annabelle! Annabelle!" Daisy exclaimed. "Pet me! Where's Jack?"

Her little tail swished so hard, it became a blur. Jack, Annabelle's dog, was Daisy's best friend.

"Hi, Daisy!" Annabelle said, leaning over to pet her. "Aren't you looking cute today!"

I bit my tongue as I studied my friend. Dressed in neon pink leggings and a green and pink sweatshirt with her hair in a ponytail on top of her head, she reminded me of a lollypop. As her crimped blonde hair cascaded around her face, she pushed it away. The dozens of bracelets she wore jangled up and down her arms. She'd never outgrown the eighties. Her speech, clothes, makeup and music tastes remained firmly fixed there.

"What's going on?" I asked as she approached, then took the seat next to Adrienne.

"Oh, my gosh!" Annabelle exclaimed. "Sally came into Sage Advice and told me her chef was, like, killed!"

"Really?" Adrienne's eyes widened. "I hadn't heard that! Did you, Gina?"

I nodded. "Yes. Sally called me after she found him."

"Why in the world would she do that?" Adrienne asked.

Shaking my head, I arched an eyebrow and glanced at Annabelle.

"Is it Mallory?" she gasped. "Is Sally worried that Mallory is going to arrest her for the murder?"

I nodded.

"She is such a jerk," Annabelle shouted as she pounded her fist onto the arm of the chair. "Anyone with half a brain cell would know that Sally couldn't kill anyone!"

"I agree," I said.

"I mean, remember when Mallory said you killed your ex-husband?" Annabelle asked.

"Yes, I do." I'd even spent some time in jail for it.

"Well, I believed that for a hot second. I think—"

"Wait a minute," I interrupted as I set

down my foot scrubber. "What do you mean you believed that I killed my ex-husband for a hot second?"

Annabelle rolled her eyes. "You kind of give off that vibe sometimes, Gina. Like, you could easily get angry enough to knock off someone."

"So you thought I killed Ralph?"

"Only for a minute!" Annabelle clarified. "It was just a quick thought! Once I got my wits about me, of course I knew you didn't!"

I narrowed my gaze. "I can't believe you're saying this."

"Gina, if I thought you had killed that jerk, would I have broken into his house and stolen all that money?"

"What!?" Adrienne shrieked. "What are you talking about?"

She hadn't been living in Heywood at that time, and Annabelle's burglary was a closely held secret.

"It's nothing." I smiled reassuringly. "It's long past history. Nothing to worry about."

Silence settled over us as I picked up the scrubber and returned to my duties, still unable to believe Annabelle thought I was capable of murder. Well, I had threatened the jerk many times, and I'd actually dreamed about ending his life. Maybe if he'd pushed me far enough, I would've killed him. But what would the limit have been? He was abusive, didn't pay child support after the divorce and rarely saw his son. Even after separating, he'd never been pleasant to me, which had been expected after our tumultuous marriage. What would've been the line I crossed into murder? Maybe self-defense?

"But, anyway," Annabelle continued. "Everyone knows Sally would never hurt anyone."

I nodded. "We can agree on that."

Moments later, I decided to let the two women know that the victim's wife would be arriving soon. They gasped just as the chimes sounded.

The three of us glanced at the door as Whitney Maven strolled in. Shiny black hair hung down her back like a curtain. She stared at her phone for a second, then looked up. I smiled and waved her over.

"Are you Whitney?" I asked. Of course, I knew exactly who she was because I'd seen her while I'd been hiding under the table at the scene of her husband's murder.

"Yes."

"Have a seat," I said.

Adrienne didn't try to hide her shock. With wide eyes, her mouth hung open in a perfect O. Meanwhile, Annabelle stared at Whitney. I could practically hear the proverbial hamster on the wheel as she tried to figure out how to bring up the woman's dead husband while Whitney typed on her phone and sat down.

I started the water and Whitney slipped off her shoes. Annabelle sat back, her gaze sliding over to the woman's device.

"How are you today?" I asked Whitney. "I'm Gina, by the way. That's Annabelle, and this is Adrienne. Annabelle owns Sage Advice, while Adrienne owns Never Quit Wining."

Whitney grunted in reply, her gaze never leaving her phone.

"It's... it's nice to meet you," Adrienne stammered. "I think I've seen you around before."

"Probably," Whitney said. "It's a small town."

Silence settled over us as I put the final touches on Adrienne's feet. Annabelle chewed on the side of her thumb while she glanced from me and back to Whitney's phone. Something had caught her attention.

"So, does anyone know when On The River is supposed to open again?" Annabelle asked.

Whitney slowly lowered her phone to her lap as I shook my head. Where was Annabelle going to take this conversation?

"I was hoping they've solved the murder there," she continued. "I love Sally's food."

"That was my husband," Whitney blurted. "He was the one who was killed."

Annabelle gasped and laid her hand over her heart. "My word! I had no idea!"

"I'm sorry for your loss," Adrienne said while squirming in her chair, obviously quite uncomfortable. "Are we done here?"

"Yes." I pushed my stool away and stood, stretching my arms over my head. "Let's get you checked out."

After she slipped on her flip flops, I followed her over to the cash register and rang her up. She handed me the credit card then whispered, "Let me know what you find out."

I smirked as I ran her card. She'd been so uncomfortable when she discovered Whitney was coming in, but she certainly was curious about the murder case.

Adrienne left and I returned to the bowls to find Annabelle and Whitney deep in conversation.

"I'm just leaving town," Whitney said. "I'm going to stay with my sister. That's who I was texting just now. I need to get out of here."

"Have they found out who killed your husband?" I asked. I sat in my stool and rolled over to her.

"No. The sheriff said she thought Sally might have done it."

"What do you think?" I asked, concentrating on her feet. It was apparent she hadn't had a pedicure in a long time.

"I don't know what to think," she sighed. "Mario told me and our neighbor, Danny, that Sally was always leaving money in the store overnight, so I think Mario got caught up in a robbery." She shook her head. "I just want to forget about my time here."

"It must be so hard to, like, lose someone you love like that," Annabelle said.

"Yes, it is."

"How long have you lived here?" I asked.

"About five or six months," Whitney replied.

At the restaurant, Whitney had claimed Mario was cheating on her, and they were divorcing. Would she mention that to us?

"Where does your sister live?" Annabelle asked.

"Colorado."

"When are you thinking of leaving?" I asked.

"As soon as I can. I have to get the house on the market, then I'm out of here."

I was surprised the police had given her the

okay to leave town. Or maybe she hadn't bothered to ask permission.

"That seems like a bit of a rash decision," Annabelle said. "What about a burial?"

Whitney snorted and shook her head. "Look, I loved the guy, but he was stepping out on me. I was leaving him anyway. The only difference is now I get the full proceeds from the house."

So far, everything was jiving with what she'd told the cops at the murder scene.

If she'd been living in Heywood six months, they couldn't have a lot of equity unless they had made a large down payment. With Mario just getting out of prison, I doubted that was the case and I realized I had no idea what Whitney did for work. She had mentioned she was a pen pal to prison inmates, but that was it.

As she tossed her long black hair over her slim shoulder, I said, "Do you have a job lined up in Colorado?"

She shook her head. "I'll go back to hair modeling. There's not any work here in this Podunk town, but in Boulder, there should be plenty."

Hair modeling? How much did a hair model make?

"Well, your hair is like, totally gorgeous," Annabelle gushed. "It looks like silk."

I nodded in agreement, still surprised someone could make a living off their hair. Or could they?

Whitney's phone rang, and she answered. After a moment, her brow furrowed. "You can't do that," she hissed. "He's dead!"

Annabelle and I exchanged glances and she shifted in her seat toward Whitney—I assumed so she could hopefully hear who was on the other end of the phone call.

As she shut her eyes, Whitney pursed her lips together. "If not now, then when?"

Annabelle was leaning so far into Whitney's chair, she looked as if she may topple right over into the woman's lap.

"Okay," Whitney said. "Just keep me posted."

While Annabelle righted herself and I finished up Whitney's feet, I asked, "Is everything okay?"

"I don't know," she sighed. "That phone call just put a crimp in my plans."

"Sorry to hear that," Annabelle said. "I hope everything gets worked out."

After Whitney had paid and exited the building, I turned to Annabelle. "What was that all about?"

"Oh, my gosh, Gina!" she yelled, bouncing

in the chair. "Guess who that was on her phone!"

"I have no idea," I said, placing my hands on my hips. "That's why I'm asking you."

"It was an insurance company!"

Where was this leading?

"And what did they say? Could you hear them?"

"They said they wouldn't be paying out on Mario's death until the murderer was behind bars!"

I nodded, slowly returned to the bowls and sat down next to her. "So Mario had a life insurance policy."

"Yes!"

"And Whitney was apparently the beneficiary."

"Yes! Oh, my gosh, Gina!"

"And Mario was cheating on her, so they were divorcing anyway."

"I'll bet you a hundred dollars she did it," Annabelle said. We sat in silence for a long moment. "Okay, not a hundred dollars, but I'll be you a dollar. I think it was Whitney."

It was a possibility, but there were other suspects I liked better. Even though Mario had cheated on Whitney, I didn't think she had the strength to make such a mess off the restaurant, lay her husband over a table and stab him.

CHAPTER 9

I PULLED into the driveway to find Trevor sitting on my porch swing with Zeus lying at his feet. Both seemed content. At least he hadn't "lost" the Golden while hiking.

"How was your day?" Trevor asked as Daisy and I exited the car. Zeus didn't even rise, but his tail slowly dusted the porch.

"Trevor! Trevor!" Daisy yelled while bounding up the porch. "Pet me! I'm a much better dog than stupid Zeus!"

"Good." I leaned over and stroked the Golden. "Whitney Maven came into the store."

"Oh really? What did she have to say?"

"Want to come in for a bit and I'll tell you about it?"

"Yes, ma'am."

Trevor stood and I unlocked the door.

Zeus headed for the couch while Daisy ran from one room to the other, taking the time to spin around in a circle in the living room before repeating. Being cooped up in the store must have left her with extra energy, giving her a good case of the zoomies.

I poured Trevor and me a glass of water and we sat at the kitchen table. After getting some water too, Daisy finally settled at my feet while gently panting. "How did things go today?" I asked.

"Great. He loved being on the trail. We did ten miles, so he should be worn out."

"I hope it lasts a couple of days," I said. "Thanks again for taking him."

"Anytime. It was nice to be out in nature and away from the ugliness of Mario's murder." He took a sip of his drink. "I definitely needed the day off, but I'm ready to get back in the saddle. Tell me what Whitney said."

"Well, she's leaving. Going to Colorado as she mentioned to revive her career as a hair model."

Trevor furrowed his brow. "Hair model? I had no idea there was such a thing."

"I didn't either, and I wonder how much one can make in that profession."

"Did you look it up?"

I shook my head. "I was busy today. Didn't have time."

Trevor pulled out his phone. We huddled together and stared at the screen. "Hair model salaries run from forty-nine thousand to a hundred thousand in the United States," Trevor read. He scrolled down a bit. "In Phoenix, they start at sixteen dollars an hour."

"What about Colorado?"

"Looks like twenty-five."

"I can't imagine you could get full time work doing that," I said. Sitting back against the chair, I crossed my arms over my chest. "It seems more of a side gig to me."

"Maybe. Why does any of it matter?"

"Well, she's going to live with her sister in Colorado and work as a hair model. She's also the beneficiary of Mario's life insurance."

Trevor arched his eyebrows and took a long sip of water. "How in the world did you come across that little piece of information?"

"Like I said, she was at File It Away today. She took a phone call, and Annabelle was listening in. It was the insurance company saying they'd need more time to process the claim... they wanted to wait until there was an arrest."

"She filed quickly," Trevor muttered.

"And she wants to be paid immediately. She made that very clear, and became angry when they put her off. I was thinking that she'd make a few bucks as a hair model, but she's also got a large insurance payout coming, so she doesn't have to worry about money."

"Don't forget about the house," Trevor said.

"I can't imagine there's much equity in it. When they purchased it, he'd just gotten out of prison and she was a hair model making sixteen bucks an hour."

"Good point," he sighed. "Do you remember the name of the insurance company?"

"Annabelle saw it on Whitney's screen," I said, pulling out my own phone. "I made a note of it in here."

After giving him the name, I shoved the phone back in my pocket.

"Interesting," Trevor said. "Good work, super sleuth."

"There was something else she said that caught my attention."

"What was that?"

"It was so quick, it barely registered. But she said that Mario had been telling her and *their neighbor* that Sally was keeping a lot of cash at the store."

"Does this neighbor have a name?"

"She called him Danny," I said. Me revealing these details to Trevor gave me anxiety simply because as someone who lived by lists and schedules, it really bothered me he wasn't taking any notes. "Do you want a piece of paper?" I asked.

"That would be helpful."

My jitters subsided as I stood and walked over to my kitchen drawer where I kept several notebooks, all with pens attached. I pulled one out and set it in front of him.

"Thanks." He opened it and I carefully studied what he wrote, making sure he didn't forget any details I'd shared. "Did she even hint she thought Danny may be responsible for the killing?"

"No. Like I said, it came and went so fast in the conversation, I barely caught it."

"I'm surprised Sally kept large amounts of money at On The River," Trevor said, drawing a dollar sign, then a question mark next to it. "She seems so responsible."

"Agreed. I can't imagine her doing that either, but I think we need to ask her about it, and then also find this Danny guy."

"Isn't there a song called Danny Guy?" Trevor asked.

"No. That's Danny Boy."

He tapped his pen against the paper. "You have Sally's number, right?"

I nodded.

"Let's call her and see what she says about this money issue."

I dialed, set the phone to speaker, then laid it on the table.

"Hi, Gina," Sally answered. "What's up? Did you find the killer and shame all the idiots at the sheriff's office yet?"

I glanced at Trevor who rolled his eyes. "Not yet," I replied. "But I'm working on it. I'm actually sitting here with one of the idiots right now, and we have some questions."

After a long moment of silence, Sally cleared her throat, then said, "Well, I wish you would've led with that."

"Hey, Sally," Trevor said.

"I'm sorry I called you an idiot."

"Let's not worry about that right now," he said. "You can make it up to me with some of that apple pie I like so much, okay?"

"Deal. What do you two want to know?"

"I saw Whitney Maven today," I began. "She mentioned that Mario said you kept large sums of money at the restaurant overnight, and she was thinking Mario may have been killed because someone knew about it and decided to rob you."

"Except for a few employees, I'm not sure who would know about that," Sally replied.

"But Mario would have?"

"Yes. He was often with me at closing."

I shut my eyes and rubbed my temples. Had Mario been killed because he'd blabbed about Sally's money to the wrong person?

"Why did you keep large sums at the store?" Trevor asked.

"Because I often leave late at night," Sally replied. "I didn't want to be walking around in the dark with a lot of cash on me. Most of the time, I go to the bank immediately after it opens the next day."

"Did you have any money missing after Mario's death?" Trevor asked.

I felt this was something that should've been explored at the murder scene, but what did I know? I was a dog rescuer, not a cop.

"Yes, I did," Sally said. "I had someone come in to put a deposit down for catering a wedding, and they paid in cash. I also had a couple of days' cash receipts. I hadn't made it to the bank."

"How much did they steal?" I asked, bile rising in my throat for my friend.

"About fifteen thousand, total," Sally said. "They took everything. I told Mallory about it when she first arrived after I'd found the body. That was my thought—that Mario had been killed while trying to stop a robbery."

Oh, my word. How would Sally recover from this?

I glanced at Trevor. "You didn't arrive at the scene with Mallory?"

He shook his head. "I was about a half-hour behind her."

"Sally, you told Mallory you thought it was a robbery gone wrong, and she decided you were the number one suspect because you shared that you and Mario fought the night before and you were the last one to leave him at the restaurant?"

"Exactly," Sally huffed. "Someone needs to run against her and get her out of office."

"I agree," I said. "Maybe Trevor here should take her on."

"Maybe you two should get back to discussing Mario's murder," he replied.

"What do you think about the other employees who know about the money you keep there?" I asked. "Would any of them be that bold to kill Mario for it?"

I could hear Sally breathing as she considered my question. Finally, she replied, "No. Both are women. There was too much violence in the restaurant. Mario was a big guy and I don't think a regular woman could take him on like that."

Unfortunately, Sally was wrong. Growing

up with an older brother, I'd learned to fight and I'd taken down some big men in my younger days. Had it been easy? No. But with the right skills, it was doable.

"I don't think that my money had anything to do with the murder," Sally continued. "It was the drugs. My guess is that they came for the drugs and the drug money, and my stash was a bonus."

Pursing my lips, I stared at the phone. She seemed so sure of herself, and I realized we had many different motives for murder. Had Mario been caught in the wrong place at the wrong time and tried to stop someone from robbing Sally? Or had it been a drug related killing? Or had his past caught up with him and Billy Hoffman, the man Mario had gone to prison for almost killing, exacted his revenge? Not to mention Mario getting Hornet, or Harry Dingle, more time in prison...

"Okay, thanks a lot, Sally," Trevor said.

"Sure. You two take care."

After Trevor disconnected the call, he picked it up and began typing.

"What are you searching for?" I asked.

"I know Mario and Whitney's address, so I thought I'd poke around the records and see if one of their neighbors goes by Danny, or something close."

Daisy snored under the table while he scrolled.

"Got it," he said, meeting my gaze. "Daniel Chavez lives next door. I think we should pay him a visit and see how he feels about Mario dying."

"When?" I asked.

"How about right now?"

I stood and glanced into the living room. Zeus still slept soundly.

Daisy lifted her gaze to me. "If you're going anywhere, you're taking me. I'm not staying here alone with him. I don't want to get blamed for anything bad he may do."

Should I trust the retriever to mind his manners? Balling my hands at my sides, I fumed. It irritated me that my whole world now revolved around him. "How long do you think we'll be there?" I asked.

"Not long," Trevor replied. "We're just stopping by for a chat to get a pulse on him."

"You aren't leaving me here," Daisy warned again.

"Okay," I said. "Let's go and see what Danny Chavez has to say. Maybe we can have this murder wrapped up by bedtime."

Trevor snorted as he stood.

"We also need to take Daisy with us," I

said. "I don't feel comfortable leaving her here with Zeus alone."

"Fair enough."

We took Trevor's truck and made our way to Danny's, which wasn't too far from my house. In Heywood, nothing was too far away, but I was surprised by just how close I lived to a potential murderer.

Daisy jumped from the car after we'd arrived. As she trotted up the walkway to the front door, I sighed, simply too tired to call her back and make her wait in the car.

Trevor and I followed her. While he knocked, I glared at her.

"What?" she said. "I'm the one with the super sniffer. I should be involved in every step of this investigation."

A variety of comebacks sat on the tip of my tongue, but all would have to wait until we were alone.

When a man answered the door—who I assumed to be Danny—I gasped and stepped back.

"Hang on a minute," Trevor said, holding his hands in front of him. "What do you need that thing for?"

Neither of us had expected him to be brandishing a gun at his side.

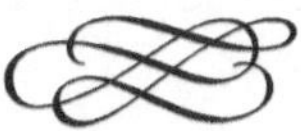

THE SHORT, muscular man in his thirties with thick black hair glared at Trevor and me, while I focused on the weapon.

"Who are you?" he asked.

"We just have a few questions about your neighbor, Mario Maven," Trevor said. "You can put the gun down."

I swallowed past my fear as Danny's gaze danced between Trevor and me.

"Aren't you a cop?" he asked Trevor.

"Yeah, I am. That's one reason of many I'd like you to put the gun down."

Danny nodded, stepped inside, then came out to the porch and shut the door behind him, without the weapon. "Sorry about that. I don't like strangers showing up at my door," he said. "There's been some bad people hanging around the neighborhood and it makes me nervous."

I sighed with relief as Daisy sniffed his shoes. After a moment, she came over and sat at my feet, but her stare remained focused on Danny's.

"Bad people?" Trevor asked.

"Yeah." He nudged his chin to his right. "Bad neighbors bring bad people."

"Isn't that where Mario and Whitney live?" Trevor asked, even though he already knew the answer.

"Yeah."

"Did you know he died?" Trevor asked.

"I heard about it," Danny said. "But wasn't he murdered? That's what the paper said."

"Yeah, he was. Can I ask you a couple of questions about him?"

Danny shrugged. "Sure."

"You knew Mario worked at On The River, right?"

"Yeah. Heard he was a great cook."

"Did you socialize with him often?"

"Man, I tried not to," Danny said, shaking his head. "I knew from the second I met him he was bad news."

"Why do you say that?" I asked.

Danny turned to me and sighed. "I grew up in Phoenix around the gangs. I can smell trouble a mile away. My wife and I moved up here to live a quiet, honest life."

"And when Whitney and Mario moved in, you felt they were bad people?" I asked.

"Yeah. Prison changes people," Danny continued. "They become jittery—always looking around like they're waiting to get jumped. I saw it with my brother when he got out of prison, and I knew it within minutes of meeting Mario. He'd done a stretch, and I didn't like him moving in."

Danny had made it perfectly clear he didn't approve of his neighbors. But did he dislike Mario enough to kill him?

"Did Mario ever talk about his job at all?" Trevor asked.

"All the time," Danny said. "I tried to avoid him, but sometimes I got caught up in conversation with him. He'd tell me about specials the restaurant was running, or maybe a story about a customer who hadn't liked the food and how angry that made him."

"Did he ever mention the owner?" I asked.

"Yeah. What's her name?" He snapped his fingers while staring at the sky, as if he'd find the answer there. "Sally. He liked her, but he did tell me she was a tough boss."

"Anything else about her?" I urged.

He shook his head, placing his hands on his waist.

"What about the business?" Trevor asked. "Did he mention anything about it?"

Danny's eyes lit up. "Yeah. He told me he was running drugs out the back, and if I ever needed anything, he could hook me up. He also said Sally wasn't very smart for leaving big amounts of money around after closing."

Trevor and I exchanged glances. Danny knew about the drugs *and* the money. I glanced at his tidy home. No paint cracks, the yard was simple and well-kept. The house didn't scream financial troubles.

"What do you do for a living, Danny?" Trevor asked.

"I work out at the recycling plant between here and Sedona," he replied. "I'm a manager out there."

"Does your wife work?" I asked.

He shook his head. "We've got two young ones. She stays home with them. I learned growing up without a father around that family is the most important thing."

"Where was your dad?" I asked.

"From the time I was four until I turned seventeen, he was in prison," Danny said.

"I'm sorry to hear that," Trevor said.

"Yeah, me too. My mom worked herself to

the bone to provide for us, and sometimes that wasn't enough. I remember more than one occasion when me and my brother went to bed hungry while my loser father was getting three square meals a day." He shook his head. "I promised myself I'd never do that to my kids."

He did seem to live a simple life. Nothing extraordinary stood out to me, but I also knew that things were very tight for us normal folks. The cost of everything had skyrocketed, and if I, as a single woman, felt the pinch, I imagined to a family, it was a lot more painful.

"Are you glad Mario's gone?" Trevor asked.

"Heck, yes!" Danny exclaimed. "Like I said, there were a lot of bad people hanging around his house."

"Whitney is also moving," I offered. "Are you happy about that?"

"She's just as bad as him," Danny replied. "Dirty as they come. A total grifter."

"Why do you say that?" I asked.

"Because of the people they kept company with," Danny said. "If I brought home bikers and ex-cons, my wife would take the kids and I'd never see her again. Remember, I grew up around all that. I know what that life can do to a person." He glanced at the Mavens' house. "Maybe a nice family with a couple of kids will move in."

I glanced down at Daisy, who had been uncharacteristically quiet. Her gaze bobbed between the three of us as she followed the conversation.

"Where were you the night Mario was murdered?" Trevor asked.

Danny shook his head and smirked. "I should've known you'd think me a suspect."

"Actually, I don't," Trevor said. "I'm following my gut and attempting to rule you out."

"I was at church with my family," Danny said. "The kids were involved in a play there."

"Did you talk to anyone?" Trevor asked.

"Yeah. Minister Paul and I talked after the play for about twenty minutes. Some other parents can also vouch for me. I can get you their names if you want."

"And after the play?" Trevor asked.

"We came home, then we put the kids to bed. My wife and I watched a little television, and we were asleep by eleven at the latest."

"What did you watch?" Trevor asked.

"Remember the *Terminator* movies?"

Both Trevor and I nodded.

"One of those was on. I don't know which one it was, but Arnold was in it."

"Is your wife home right now?" I asked.

"Nope. She's with the kids. I think they

went to the grocery store. I just got home not too long ago."

I couldn't think of anything else to ask him, and I glanced at Trevor. His gaze had narrowed as he stared at Danny. "Well, thanks for your time, Mr. Chavez. I really appreciate it."

"Sure. And I'm sorry about the gun. Living next door to those two has made me paranoid as heck. Can't wait until she's gone."

"If you see anything over there, can you give me a call?" Trevor asked.

"Sure."

"I'm actually on my day off so I don't have a business card with me, but if you call the Sheriff's department, they can patch you through to my cell phone if I'm out of the office."

"Will do," Danny said.

Trevor, Daisy and I returned to the car.

"I wish you had brought a notepad," I said, desperately trying to mentally hang on to every detail I'd heard.

"Me, too," Trevor said.

As he started the car, I opened the glove box, then the middle console looking for a pen and something to write on.

Trevor gently tapped my arm. "Check this out."

I glanced up to see a shiny black truck

pulling into the driveway. A moment later, two kids scrambled out the back and a woman exited the driver's side. I didn't get a good look at her as I was too busy staring at where the license plate should be. Instead, a white piece of paper took its place, indicating the truck was newly purchased.

When the three had entered the house, Trevor drove away.

"So, let's recap," Trevor said. "Danny admits he knew about the money at Sally's. And he disliked Mario and Whitney."

"He also comes from a sketchy background," I said. "It sounds like he was around a lot of violence growing up."

"But he's turned himself around," Trevor said.

"That's what he's telling you, but is it true?"

"I don't know," Trevor said. "I'll have to do a little digging into his past."

"There's no sense talking to his wife. For all we know, he's in their house telling her she needs to give him an alibi for that night."

"I agree, but we can talk to Minister Paul. If he had a conversation with Danny, he should remember."

"And he won't lie for Danny, either," I said.

"At least, I hope he won't. That wouldn't be very godly."

"Can we discuss that truck for a minute?" I turned to face Trevor as he drove. "That thing was new."

"No, I think that was a 2018."

"Then it was new to them," I said. I couldn't tell a Chevy from a Volkswagen, let alone pinpoint what year a car was manufactured. "It still had the dealer paper where the license plate should've been."

"Really? I didn't notice."

"Yes!" I exclaimed. "And fifteen thousand dollars would make an excellent down payment!"

"If not buy the thing outright," Trevor muttered. "Harry down at Tinkering on Trucks has had some trucks for sale in his lot. I'll have to talk to him and see if he sold one, and when."

"Good idea," I said. "Danny plays innocent, but it could be all an act. He's got the background to know exactly what to say to make himself likeable and place the blame elsewhere."

We rode in silence for a few moments, then Trevor said, "I'm trying to figure out how this went down. He knew about the money at Sally's and decided to rob the place. Mario was there to try to stop him. They fought. Danny has no problem killing Mario because he doesn't like him. Then he gets the money and the drugs, and heads home ready to place the blame on the sketchy people he sees over at Mario's house."

"And then he went and bought a new truck," I said.

"Gina?" Daisy's soft voice came from the back seat.

I turned.

"That man? Danny? I also smelled him at the restaurant."

"What?" I screeched.

"What do you mean what?!" Trevor shouted. "What the heck is going on!"

"I... I thought I saw a rabbit running into the road!" I cried, facing forward.

"Don't do that, Gina!" Trevor said, taking a few deep breaths.

"I'm sorry." I pulled down my visor and glanced at Daisy in the mirror.

"When we were at the restaurant, I caught Danny's scent," Daisy said, meeting my gaze. "He'd been there."

CHAPTER 11

TREVOR and I rode the rest of the way in silence. When he dropped Daisy and me off at home, I refrained from saying anything to her until we were safely inside and no one could hear our conversation.

"Why in the world didn't you tell me you smelled Danny at the restaurant while we were talking to him?" I asked, leaning against the front door. "I could've asked him more questions!"

Daisy sat down facing me, her big brown eyes staring up at me. "Because I'm trying to be a good girl and I didn't want to interrupt you. You don't like it when I do that."

Narrowing my gaze, I crossed my arms over my chest. "You've never cared that I don't like you interrupting me before."

"I know, but Zeus is such a bad dog, and I don't want to be like him. I'm trying to be *better* than him."

Speaking of which, where was he?

I hurried into the living room to find the couch empty. The kitchen was still intact. "He's got to be in here somewhere," I muttered as I ran down the hall with Daisy at my heels. "I should've locked him in the laundry room."

Nothing in Jacob's room. Hall bathroom was clear.

"He must have invaded *our* bedroom," Daisy said.

We found Zeus on the bed chewing on the remains of my slipper. He didn't bother to hide it, and as my gaze met his, I realized he had no shame, either. No downcast eyes, no curling his tail between his legs. Instead, he boldly stared at me with the mangled fabric hanging from his mouth.

"Okay," I sighed. "Give me the slipper."

He hopped from the bed and ran from the room. Before chasing him, I jotted down *order slippers* on my to-do list. Then I strode down the hall to retrieve my destroyed footwear.

I found the Golden on the couch, my slipper dangling from his mouth.

"Drop it," I ordered.

To my utter shock, he did.

"Good boy," I said, giving him a good scratch behind the ear. "Somewhere in there are some manners."

"He's making sense when he talks, too," Daisy interjected. "He said he's sorry and doesn't like being alone."

I sat down on the couch next to him, gently stroking his head. When he laid his chin down on my knee, I leaned back against the cushions. "I'm feeling bad that I had to leave you," I said. "Sometimes dogs need to be left alone."

He inched forward, placing his paws on my thighs.

"You know, I've only chewed up a sock and you yelled at me for a long time," Daisy huffed. "I didn't get snuggles like you're giving the great golden goober."

"Have a little compassion, Daisy."

She sighed and left the room. Zeus was now almost lying across my lap. Sitting up, he licked my face, then placed his paws on my shoulders and settled against me.

Eighty pounds of golden fluff in my face wasn't what I expected. "Okay, buddy. Please get down now."

When he didn't move, I tried to manhandle him off me, but he had me pinned to the couch.

"You're suffocating me," I said, spitting some hair out of my mouth. In my sternest voice, I yelled, "Off! Now!"

He didn't move as he stared down at me, and I had no idea how I'd get out from under him.

"Come on, Zeus," I whined, shoving his chest. "Please get off me."

I made a little progress. After a long moment, he jumped off, then I stood from the couch and went to the kitchen to open the door to the backyard. "Why don't you go dig holes?" I suggested.

He ran outside and I slammed the door, then returned to my bedroom where I found Daisy curled up on the bed.

I fired up the computer after scratching her behind the ears.

Closing my eyes, I took a few deep breaths and wondered if that beast would try to suffocate me in my sleep. Did I have a monster on my hands, or just a misunderstood dog? And if the latter was the case, what should I do to connect with him and set the boundaries he so desperately wanted to break?

Exercise definitely seemed to help, so whoever adopted him would have to be quite active. And he didn't like to be alone, so maybe I could find someone who worked from home?

I turned back to my computer and sent an email off to the author who was looking for me to write another mystery for her. "I've got a doozy for you," I muttered as I typed. Then I outlined a few chapters which included a murder at a restaurant, bikers, ex-cons and a shady wife. I debated whether to make her a hair model or not, but I jotted it down with a question mark.

My next call was to the vet in Sedona. Since I'd been in so many times with my rescues, we'd developed a good relationship. Even the receptionist knew me. She said she'd have Dr. Picote call me back when he had a free minute.

I set down my phone and thought about the case again. Just because Daisy smelled Danny in the restaurant didn't necessarily mean anything. A lot of people ate there. His scent could've been from days ago.

"Do you think that was a fresh scent you caught at the restaurant?" I asked, turning to her.

"It seemed pretty strong," Daisy said. "I don't know how old it was, though."

"Where did you smell it?" I asked.

She rolled over onto her back and stuck all four feet up in the air. "By the table where you left me when you went into the kitchen."

That had been somewhat close to the

murder scene. Perhaps Danny had walked around the restaurant after the killing, looking for more to steal? Or maybe he and his little family had eaten there and just so happened to sit at that table, or one near it?

"I should've asked him if he frequented On The River," I murmured.

"You should have done that," Daisy agreed.

"I didn't even think of it until you brought up that little detail."

"Sorry, Gina. I was just trying to be a good girl."

"You are a good girl," I said. I moved to the bed and lay down next to her so we were face to face. "I love you. You're perfect just the way you are."

"Sometimes you get mad at me. Like when I don't come when you call me."

"Yeah, that does irritate me."

"And sometimes I sniff too long in one spot when we are on our walks."

"Yes, you do."

"And then you got mad when I threw up on the carpet."

"Well, next time try to hit the tile, okay?"

"Then there was that one time—"

"Daisy, you aren't a bad dog," I interrupted as I reached out and stroked her belly.

"I'm afraid you'll think I'm as horrible as Zeus."

"Are you going to start acting like Zeus?"

She sighed and rolled to her side so her paws pressed into my stomach. "I don't think I can be as bad as Zeus even if I tried."

I kissed her nose and smiled. "Exactly."

"What's wrong with his brain, Gina?"

"I have no idea," I sighed. "Maybe Dr. Picote will be able to tell us."

"Are you going to make me go see the vet?"

"No."

"Do you promise?"

"Yes, I promise."

"Good. I don't like him."

"I've never met a dog who does, Daisy."

"He sticks that thing up my butt."

"It's to check your temperature."

"Well, you shouldn't let him do that to me. I'll tell you if I'm hot."

We lay staring at each other for a long while. I debated a nap, but decided against it. Dinnertime was right around the corner, and I had other things to do before settling in for the evening. An early bedtime would have to suffice.

I rose from the bed and did a little more work on my outline. About twenty minutes had passed when Daisy said, "Would Sally know if Danny has recently been eating at her restaurant?"

After setting down my pen, I cursed. Why hadn't I thought of that? "That's a good idea. If he paid via credit card, she'll have a record of it."

"Maybe he went there to eat and was casing the place, figuring out the best way to rob her."

I stared at my dog for a long moment. When had she become smarter than me? Or was I basically talking to myself during these conversations? Everyone knew dogs couldn't speak...

I picked up my phone and dialed Sally.

"Hi, Gina. What's up?"

"Do you know who Danny Chavez is?"

"I... I don't think so. Should I?"

"Probably not," I said. "But I was wondering if you could look through your receipts for a week or two before the murder and see if you have any record of him."

Sally was quiet for so long, I wondered if she'd hung up. Finally, she asked, "Why?"

I shut my eyes, wishing I'd thought through the phone call a little better before dialing. Telling Sally my dog caught his scent wasn't going to work.

"Just a silly thought," I said.

"If it's so silly, then why are you asking me to go through the receipts?"

I rubbed my finger between my eyebrows. "If my silly idea pans out, we may catch the killer, Sally."

"That would be great, but I feel like you need to share this thought process with me."

I'm not ready to divulge all the information yet." I snorted and laughed. "In fact, my reasoning is a little embarrassing."

"Gina, you caring what people think of you is new."

She had a point. I'd never been concerned before and it was out of character for me to start now. "You know what? You're right. Please forget I even called. It's dumb and I'm grasping at straws."

"Gina—"

"It's okay, Sally. Don't worry about it."

I hung up and stared at my phone.

"Why would you tell her not to worry about it?" Daisy asked. "He might be the killer!"

"Yes, you're right. But I'm hoping that maybe my little reverse psychology and secrecy will spur her on to check the receipts."

Daisy giggled. "Aren't you clever."

"Every now and then, yes."

Both Daisy and I jumped when someone pounded on the front door.

As I walked down the hall to answer, I also heard Zeus barking. I stopped at the kitchen to let him in, and he immediately ran to the front door.

I gasped as I took in my visitor.

"This doesn't look good," Daisy said as Zeus continued to bark.

CHAPTER 12

BEFORE ME STOOD a six-foot plus man with a black Mohawk, a matching beard, and tattoos covering his muscular arms. When a small smile parted his lips, I realized he was missing a front tooth. He wore jeans and a sleeveless red and blue flannel shirt that pulled against his girth.

He slowly removed his sunglasses. "Gina?"

I nodded and tried to hush the dogs. "I'm guessing you're Hornet," I said above the din.

"How did you know?" he asked, his brow furrowing in confusion.

"Well, that hornet tattooed on the side of your neck is a dead giveaway."

His smile broadened. "Handlebar told me you wanted to see me."

"Yes, but I didn't expect you to show up unannounced at my house." I pulled Zeus's collar so that he stood between me and the big man. Would he protect me if Hornet tried to hurt me? I had my doubts. He'd probably stand by and watch, maybe even cheer him on, if he could talk.

"I'm on my way out of town," he said. "Thought I'd do you a solid and come by before I left."

As I studied Hornet's—or Harry Dingle's—face, I looked for any signs that he was here to beat the living tar out of me, or worse. My gut told me he was safe, and most likely Handlebar had conveyed he was to leave me as he found me, even if I was questioning whether he was a murderer or not.

Growing up with Vic as my brother and watching his friends and acquaintances come and go had left me with a pretty good meter of reading people. It had become my sixth sense. Not that Hornet was actually a good person, but I felt he didn't have any ulterior motives for being at my house. He was fulfilling Handlebar's request.

"Take a seat," I said, pointing to the porch swing. "I'll be right back."

Daisy followed me while Zeus stood between Hornet and the door. As Hornet moved to the swing, Zeus inched forward, showing his protective instincts. Or maybe my surprise guest had a ham sandwich in his pocket—either way, the Golden had taken an interest in him.

I hurried down the hall to the bedroom, grabbed my little revolver out of the nightstand, shoved it into my sweatshirt pocket, then returned to the porch. I may have thought Hornet's motives for being at my house were legitimate, but I wasn't stupid. I'd protect myself at all costs.

I leaned against the railing facing the hulking man, who was gently swaying back and forth on my swing. Frankly, I didn't blame him for changing his name. The Harry Dingle moniker didn't do him any favors and didn't match his exterior.

"What if that swing breaks?" Daisy asked. "He's too big for it."

She wasn't wrong. I cleared my throat and hoped it held. Hornet breaking the swing into a million pieces could be the event that shifted his mood.

"So, what do you want to know?" he asked. "I've got nothing to hide."

I hated small talk, so diving right in was good with me.

"You were in prison with Mario Maven, is that correct?"

"Yep."

"And he snitched on you and you received an extra sentence, right?"

"Yes, ma'am."

I had to be careful with my next question because I didn't want to get Handlebar in trouble. "Word is around town that you were in Sedona saying you wanted revenge on him for what he did."

"Yes. I said that."

"So you did want to kill him?"

"I sure did."

The conversation seemed too easy. I'd expected more resistance to my questions. "And did you go through with that threat?"

He shook his head. "No," he stated firmly.

"Are you sure?"

He threw his head back and laughed. "Trust me, I'd remember if I killed someone."

"I would hope so," I mumbled. "You didn't get your revenge then, did you?"

He nodded. "I most certainly did."

"But you just said you didn't kill him," I stated, furrowing my brow. "I'm confused."

"Look, I was up in Sedona—I know some of the guys in the biker gang. We were hanging out and I was asking around about drugs, who the players were in the area. Handlebar mentioned that he knew a guy in Heywood who was dealing. Handlebar was supplying. We got to talking, and I realized that this Mario Maven character he was mentioning was that weasel Peter Smith who did me dirty in prison, and was living a new life in this nice, little town with a pretty, little wife. I had a few beers by then, so I started running my mouth, making that threat."

"But you didn't go through with it."

"Nah." He stretched his arms across the back of the swing. "I just got out of prison, Gina. I don't want to chance going back in."

He didn't meet my gaze, and I wasn't sure if he was being truthful.

"If you had to guess who killed Mario... or Peter, whatever you want to call him, who do you think it was?" I asked.

"I have no idea," Hornet said. "I remember Handlebar saying that Petey owed him money. Maybe he offed him."

Since I'd known Handlebar for years, I wasn't sure if he was murdering material, but I also believed that everyone had a dark side. When the right proverbial buttons were pushed, anyone could kill. I didn't like that Hornet had thrown Handlebar under the proverbial bus, though.

"Why would you say that?" I asked.

"Handlebar told me Mario owed him

money. Handlebar doesn't like it when people owe him money."

But did that make him a killer? No one liked it when they were owed money.

"I still think it was Handlebar," Daisy said. "Or maybe this guy. Or maybe even Whitney or Danny."

How helpful. She'd listed all the suspects. Yes, it could be any of them.

"Did you ever meet Mario's wife?" I asked. If he wasn't going to confess to the murder, I'd pick his brain on the other suspects Daisy had mentioned.

"I did."

"When was that?" I asked, surprised.

"Maybe a week or so before he died," Hornet replied. "Nice lady. Real pretty hair."

"How did you meet her?" I asked.

"Someone gave me their address... I can't remember who. Someone at the biker club in Sedona. I stopped by one evening and said hello. Told her I was an old friend of Petey's."

"Did you tell her you knew him in prison?"

"No. I had the feeling she'd slam the door in my face if I did. I'm sure they shared some pillow talk on what happened in prison and why he was let out a bit early."

While peppering Hornet, I'd also kept an eye on Zeus. He'd been sniffing around Hornet's shoes, and finally laid his head on the man's lap. To my shock, the big biker gently stroked him.

"This is a great dog," he said. As if on cue, Zeus put both paws on his lap. "He's a friendly fella, isn't he?"

"You have no idea," Daisy muttered. "He's such a *bad* boy."

Within seconds, Zeus had climbed onto Hornet's lap. The eighty-pound fluff ball looked down at the biker, then licked his face.

Hornet burst out laughing and rubbed the sides of his head. "You know what I missed most in prison?"

"I have no idea," I sighed. I was expecting the answer to be something like beer, women and sex.

"Dogs. I love dogs," he said. "They are better than most people."

Well, I might have more in common with the ex-con than I realized. "I agree," I sighed. "What did you and Whitney talk about?"

"The weather, how Pete was doing at the restaurant. Just small talk."

"Why in the world would you go over there?" I asked.

"Because I wanted to see what he had," Hornet said. "What he'd built since squealing on me and getting me more time in prison."

He shrugged. "It was more curiosity than any-thing. Was the snitch in prison the same man on the outside?"

As I watched the biker and the dog, I won-dered if I had a match. Zeus seemed to be en-thralled with Hornet, but I didn't think it would be a good pairing. The man had no home and was leaving town. Speaking of which...

"Where are you headed off to?" I asked.

"Michigan. I have family there."

"Why did you come to this area before heading there?"

He shrugged. "I wanted to see my boys in Sedona. They're a good group of guys."

"Didn't you have to touch base with a pa-role officer or something?"

"Yeah. I talked to my guy in Michigan al-ready and told him I had some car trouble and I was on my way."

I glanced over my shoulder at the motor-cycle parked in front of my house. Telling the parole officer he was having car issues and showing up on a motorcycle may be a problem for Hornet, but it wasn't mine to worry over.

As I struggled for more questions where I hoped I could trip him up, I realized he hadn't explained to me what his revenge had been on Mario.

"You mentioned that you got revenge on Peter," I said. "What did you do?"

Hornet chuckled. "I'm not going to say, but I didn't kill him, okay?"

After he pushed Zeus off his lap, he stood and stretched his arms over his head. "Thanks for the chat, Gina. And for letting me pet that dog. He's awesome."

"*No. He's. Not.*" Daisy said. "He's a *bad* dog. I'm the good dog here, and I wish people would remember that."

I hoped Hornet didn't disappear into the wind. If he did go to Michigan, at least Trevor could keep tabs on him through his parole officer.

But what had his revenge been?

"What did you do to get back at Mario?" I called out as he strolled across the grass to his bike.

He turned and smiled again. "Sorry, Gina. I don't kiss and tell."

I gasped, trying to figure out what he meant.

As he drove away, there was only one conclusion that made any sense: he'd slept with Mario's wife, Whitney.

CHAPTER 13

I SPENT the whole night tossing and turning. *I don't kiss and tell.* What exactly did that mean?

It could indicate that he'd either slept with a very willing Whitney... or an unwilling Whitney, and that bothered me more than I could put into words.

Had I just allowed a rapist to slip through my fingers?

"I should've pulled my gun out and shot him," I grumbled the next morning as I paced the living room with a cup of coffee in hand, the carpet tickling my bare toes. Daisy sat on the couch watching me while Zeus destroyed my other slipper. I didn't bother to stop him. "And asked questions later."

"You had already asked him a bunch of questions," Daisy said.

"I know, but I wish I'd been quicker to think about what his words meant."

"You can always ask Whitney," Daisy offered. "That would've been before the murder, right?"

"Yes, exactly."

"Well, ask her, then."

As I paced, I tried to figure out how to ask someone if they'd been sexually assaulted—a delicate subject that even the closest of friends didn't discuss. How did I approach someone I'd only spoken to once?

I didn't. It was as simple as that. "I can't ask her," I muttered, then sipped my coffee. "It's too personal."

Instead, I called Trevor and asked him if Whitney had reported a rape.

"I... I don't think so. I'll have to go through the records. Why?"

After explaining my conversation with Hornet, Trevor sighed. "Okay, I'll take a look. You said he was headed back to Michigan, right?"

"That's what he told me," I replied. "But he also said that he had no intentions of going back to jail, so I can't imagine him actually hurting Whitney."

"I'll check and let you know."

As I hung up, Zeus continued to rip apart

my footwear. I eyed him with disdain. Should I stop him? Yes. My coffee hadn't kicked in quite yet though. Energy would be needed to wrestle it from the jerk.

He began barking when someone knocked on my front door. Glancing out the window, I saw it was my dad. In his eighties, he stood on the porch waiting for me to answer. Arthritis had curved the spine of the once formidable man who had scared me whenever he raised his voice while growing up.

Heck, if he looked at me the wrong way now, my stomach clenched in fear.

With his slipper forgotten, Zeus hurried to the door.

"Who is it?" Daisy yelled. "Who's at the door? Do I need to bark in my loud, mean voice?"

"It's my dad," I said.

Pulling open the door, I placed a smile on my face.

"Gina!" he said, raising his arms wide. "How's my girl?"

"I'm fine, Dad." I fell into his embrace and the love he had for me washed over me like a cozy blanket on a cold day. There was nothing better than a hug from my dad. "Come in. I just made coffee."

"My timing is perfect," he said, smiling.

Gray hair and a matching beard framed his face while his green eyes twinkled. "Who's the new mutt?"

"His name's Zeus, and he's a jerk."

Dad leaned over and stroked his head. "That's not the greatest selling point, Gina."

"I know, but I really haven't found any good ones."

He chuckled as he followed me into the kitchen and sat down. "Every dog has a good selling point. Maybe his is that he's a good watch dog."

I pulled a cup from the cupboard then glanced at the Golden stealing a tissue out of my father's pocket. "Maybe."

As Zeus ran from the room with the tissue, I didn't bother to chase him because I had a feeling that was exactly what he wanted. Hopefully he'd chew it up enough so it passed through his digestive system without issue.

With a smile, I sat down with my dad and handed him a cup of coffee.

He took a sip while eyeing me over the rim of the cup. "Ah, that tastes good, Gina. Strong, but not like gasoline. That's how your brother likes it."

"I'm aware." When he'd stayed with me, I'd had to drink the nasty brew.

Comfortable silence fell over us, and I

found it almost as wonderful as the hug we shared. I closed my eyes and bathed in the quiet closeness.

"I talked to Vic," he said after a moment.

"How's he?"

"I'm afraid he's worried about you."

Shaking my head, I rolled my eyes. "Why? What did I do now?"

My father cupped the mug, as if he used it to warm his hands. "Well, apparently you've gotten yourself wrapped up in another murder investigation."

Oh. That little detail.

I'd been so consumed with the stupid Zeus, I hadn't even considered that poking my nose into a killing may be a little dangerous.

"That friend of yours... Sam Jones. She did the same thing," he continued. "I remember when she figured out who killed your deadbeat ex-husband and got you out of jail."

"Yes, she did," I replied. "I'll be forever grateful for that."

"I think it's best if you don't follow in her footsteps," he said. "There are too many dangerous people in this town, Gina. Vic has told me who you've been speaking to, and it has to stop. Now."

Pursing my lips, I stared at my coffee, the reflection of the light above showing in the dark liquid. Were there dangerous people in Heywood? Yes. There were dangerous people everywhere. Was I dabbling in the dark side of Heywood? Yes. But my brother had lived there for so long, I felt like I had a pass to travel and snoop around that side without issue. "I'll be fine, Dad." I reached out and patted his wrinkled hand.

He shifted his narrowed gaze to me. "You are being stupid, Gina. I didn't raise a stupid woman."

The words hit me like a slap in the face. Lifting my hand to my cheek, I slowly rubbed it as if he'd actually struck me. "What are you talking about? You didn't seem to have any problem when I was looking for who killed Vic's ex-girlfriend."

"That was different," he said gruffly. "You were protecting your family. You couldn't allow Vic to take the fall for something he didn't do."

"And now, I'm trying to help my friend, Sally," I said. "The sheriff thinks she may have killed her chef."

"She's not family."

"But she's important to me," I said. "I want to help her."

After taking a couple long gulps of his coffee, he set down the mug. "She's not family," he repeated.

"So what?" I asked. "You're starting to sound like a mob boss."

He remained quiet for a long while, his gaze focused on the wall in front of him.

"Dad? What's going on?"

"Let's just say I'm very familiar with the world you're poking your nose into. You don't belong there, Gina—and it's not safe for you."

"What are you talking about?" I asked, my breath catching in my throat. My brother was the one who used to deal drugs and get arrested. I knew nothing about my father being involved in any of it. Growing up, he'd worked many jobs, but none of them held the title of drug dealer or bad guy.

None that I knew of.

"Dad, what are you not telling me?" I asked. "What the heck is going on?"

His jaw worked while he slowly spun the coffee cup in his hands.

"I'm not good at reading between the lines," I continued. "I need to help Sally. You keep telling me I shouldn't but you're not really giving me a good reason why."

"The fact that you may be hurt is a good enough reason," he growled.

"And I have Vic for protection," I said.

"Vic is done with that life," he said. "Your relationship with him doesn't offer any protection anymore. In fact, it may make you a target."

A sinking feeling settled in my stomach and suddenly my coffee didn't taste very good as it rose in the back of my throat. "What are you talking about? A target for what? By whom?"

Closing his eyes, he shook his head. "I've always been proud that you're a strong-willed woman who questioned everything... except for right now. Now, I wish you'd just listen to me for once."

Zeus returned to the kitchen and stuck his nose in my father's pants pocket, probably searching for another tissue. When none was found, he laid his head on his leg.

My dad glanced down and smiled, then stroked the blond head for a few long moments. I waited patiently to hopefully hear the full story of why he didn't want me to find Mario's killer.

Finally, he sighed and met my gaze. "I'm not proud of my past," he said. "And I was hoping I could hide it from you and take it to my grave, but your life may be in danger. Therefore, I'm going to swallow my shame and tell you everything in the hopes that you'll mind your own dang business and quit this sleuthing nonsense you're doing."

Pursing my lips together, I sat back in my chair and crossed my arms over my chest as if they'd protect me from whatever he was going to say next. My heart thundered while my knee began to bounce. I didn't try to hide my nervousness.

"Back when you kids were young... when your mom was still around, I was one of the biggest drug runners in the state," he said. "Arizona was mine."

I stared at my father, unable to speak. What the heck? How did I not know any of this?

"I kept it hidden from you kids," he said. "I never, ever conducted business at the house."

"Did Mom know about it?" I asked.

"Yes, she did."

"What about Vic?"

"When he was in his twenties, he wanted to make some easy money, or so he thought. I'd heard through the grapevine that there was a new dealer in town. Imagine my surprise when I found out it was my son."

"What happened then?" I asked.

"He came to work for me. By then I was tired and the operation was scaled way down."

As I ran through memories of my childhood, trying to pinpoint when my father had been a local drug kingpin, nothing stood out. "Well, you did a good job keeping it from me," I replied. "I had no idea."

"Sure you did," he said. "You just didn't want to see it."

"I don't think that's right," I replied. "I literally can't recall ever questioning anything you told me."

"Think about all the jobs I had, Gina."

Okay, there had been a lot. Truck driver. Garbage man. Retail at Hammer and Nail Hardware. Working at the recycling plant.

"When I told you I was a truck driver, you asked where my truck was and if you could have a ride in it. I realized I wouldn't be able to keep that lie going for long because you were so dang persistent in getting what you wanted, but it allowed me to leave town overnight and have the neighbor watch you and Vic."

I vaguely recalled Mrs. Chester spending the night at my house every now and then when we were told my dad had to go out of town for work.

"Your brother believed everything I told him without question," he continued. "But not you. No, Gina had to question everything, making my life as a drug dealer infinitely more difficult than it should've been." He chuckled and shook his head.

There was a lot to digest there, and I wouldn't be able to do so with my father sitting across the table. He'd lied to me for many years, but I understood why. I needed to process it all and take stock of my emotions afterward. Currently, I felt numb.

I cleared my throat. "I don't understand what the past has to do with me finding out who killed Sally's chef."

"It goes back to Handlebar's father and me," he said. "Let's just say we were rivals. He actually put a hit out on me once, but back then there were boundaries that weren't crossed, like getting someone at home. He left you and Vic alone, and he didn't bother me when I was with you kids."

"I guess that was nice of him," I muttered, unable to believe my childhood had been right out of a mobster movie and I hadn't even realized it. Either my father was a master at deception or I noticed very little in my day-to-day life.

"We negotiated a truce many years ago," my dad said. "No more hits. I was looking to downscale, and he took over most of the state. I was fine with that."

"Okay, great." I sighed in frustration. "I still don't understand what this has to do with me."

"Handlebar is running things now," he said. "With Vic out, he's got control of the whole state. I have a feeling that Mario's death is connected back to him."

That was good to know. Of course, evidence would be nice, but that was more points in favor of Handlebar being the killer.

"And Gina, you messing around in their business is not right," he continued. "This has nothing to do with you. Handlebar may decide that if you're getting too close to proving he killed Mario, he could take you out of the picture, and we may never see you again—dead or alive."

CHAPTER 14

I wasn't sure what was worse: my father being a drug runner or me being in the sights of the current kingpin.

When I had been young, I'd thought my mother had left us. Had she met her demise at the hands of Handlebar's father as some sort of retaliation for a disagreement back then?

"Is that what happened to Mom?" I asked. "Was she killed?"

"I hope not," he grumbled. "Handlebar's father and I had an argument. He threatened her and I told her to leave and never come back. I don't know if she's dead or alive."

I gasped, the admission stunning me. Time seemed to stop as I stared at my father.

"Why in the world wouldn't you tell me this?" I whispered.

"How was I supposed to explain drug violence to a four-year-old?"

"But I'm in my mid-forties now," I said, spreading my arms to my side. "That's a few decades and a lot of days that you could've explained everything to me!"

"I know," he sighed. "I thought about telling you, but it was so far in the past... I just figured I'd leave it there."

The day our mother left had been seared into my mind. Vic hadn't been particularly nice to her. In fact, he'd told her she was fat and then refused to empty the dishwasher. Shortly after, she'd announced she was going to the store and we'd never seen her again.

"What about Vic?" I asked. "Does he know the truth? He thought she left because of him."

"He knows. When he got involved in the business, I had to educate him on exactly what he was getting himself into."

Well, knock me over with a feather. My own brother hadn't bothered to share this life-changing piece of information with me? What was wrong with my family?

I slammed my hand down on top of the table and Daisy yelped from under it. "Too loud! Too loud!" She barked. "I don't like loud noises!"

Reaching under, I pet her head and tried to soothe her. "Sorry about that," I murmured.

"Now you know everything," my dad said. "And you'll stop poking your nose where it doesn't belong."

He stood to leave, and I shook my head. "Sit down, please. I have more questions."

As he lowered himself back into the chair, I rose to fetch the coffee pot. I refilled both of our cups, then took a deep breath.

"Where is she?" I asked.

"I told you, I don't know."

"I'm not sure I believe that. One hour she's here, the next she's gone and you haven't heard from her since?"

"No, I haven't."

I studied his weathered face to look for any sign of him lying, but found none. However, he'd been lying to me almost my whole life, so maybe he had it down to a science.

"Really? She's never contacted you?"

He shook his head. "I told her if she wanted to live, she needed to disappear. And she did."

"Have you ever looked for her?" I asked.

"A couple of times. She's either a master at disappearing, or she's dead." He shrugged. "I just don't know which one it is."

"Did she give any indication on where she was going?"

"No."

He stood again and this time, I didn't bother to try to stop him. A feeling of disgust swirled in my gut as he walked toward the front door, Zeus at his heels.

With a long sigh, I followed, wondering if I was in shock. My brain felt numb, yet my heart raced and my palms had become sweaty.

"Find a good selling point for this dog," my dad ordered as he stroked Zeus's head. "He doesn't seem that bad."

"Tell that to Gina's slippers," Daisy grumbled.

I felt I had to say something. My father had just unraveled my life by sharing the truth, and also informed me I could be in danger. But my emotions swirled with anger and betrayal as I fisted my sweaty palms at my sides.

"Thanks for your honesty," I blurted out, but I wasn't sure if I was thankful for it in the least bit.

"Promise me you'll stop this silly investigation," my dad said. "You have no business in it."

I couldn't take that oath, so I simply smiled while crossing my fingers behind my back.

Childish, but it somehow made me feel a bit better about not keeping the promise.

"Good girl," he said. "And I'm sorry it's come to this, Gina. I'm sorry you had to find out about everything."

I was sorry as well, but at the same time, furious that I hadn't been privy to it before. Wait until I spoke with my brother. I had a few choice words for him. How dare he keep this monumental secret from me?

As my father strode down the driveway, I shut the door and leaned against it.

"I didn't understand everything, but that sounded like a pretty heavy conversation by the tone of your voices, Gina." I glanced down to find Daisy sitting at my feet, staring up at me. "What can I do to make you feel better?"

Dogs. Better than any therapeutic. I slid down to the floor and gathered her in my arms. To my surprise, tears flowed down my cheeks. I wasn't a crier, but I couldn't seem to stop them.

Zeus simply sat next to me, his gaze trained on Daisy. I hoped he minded his manners because I didn't have the energy to discipline him. He began whining, then licked my wet face.

"Back off, you blond buffoon," Daisy growled. "She's mine."

Of course, Zeus ignored her. After licking

my face again, he lay down and put his head in my lap, pushing Daisy aside just a bit.

"There's room for everyone," I sniffed.

I closed my eyes and allowed the comfort the two canines provided to wash over me. My heartbeat slowed, but the tears kept coming. I'd grown up without a mother, and I could've used one. My brother and I were wild children, almost feral. My father hadn't known how to parent, and maybe that was because he was too busy being a drug dealer.

"That's not fair," I whispered. "He did the best he could."

It would be a long time before I could forgive him, though.

My phone rang and I debated ignoring it.

"You should see who's calling," Daisy said. "Maybe it's someone who wants to adopt the dumb blond."

Since I hadn't done any advertising on him yet, I knew that wouldn't be the case. However, I wouldn't squash Daisy's hopes.

"It's the vet," I said, wiping my nose with the sleeve of my sweatshirt.

"He's going to tell you that Zeus is mentally challenged," Daisy replied. "And that we should lose him as soon as we can."

"I'm not losing the dog on purpose," I

grumbled, then answered the phone. "Hi, Dr. Picote."

"Hi, Gina," his deep voice greeted me. "What can I do for you?" He'd been a vet for over thirty years, and I appreciated his experience as well as his willingness to give me a call instead of making me come into the office. I'd been rescuing dogs for almost two decades, and we'd developed a good relationship.

I also appreciated his hatred of small talk. I didn't have the energy for it anyhow. "I found a Golden retriever tied to my front porch. He's got some behavioral issues, so I was wondering if there was such a thing as doggy ADHD."

I had to be careful with what I said because I couldn't tell him my talking dog heard Zeus talking and said his words were jumbled.

He chuckled, then sighed. "What's he doing?"

"Lack of focus, impulsiveness, destruction."

"How old is he?"

"Young. I would guess maybe two or three?"

"It sounds like he could be hyperkinetic," Dr. Picote said. "It's different from ADHD in people, but it does exist. It's somewhat odd behavior for a Golden retriever. Usually you find it in German Shepherds, Collies and Terrier breeds."

"How rare is it?" I asked.

"Last I read, it's twelve to fifteen percent of all dogs, so I would say very rare."

Of course he ended up on my porch because I didn't have enough going on. Why was the universe throwing a dog with doggy ADHD into my life? "What can I do to help him out?" I asked, stroking the golden fur while Daisy eyed me with disdain. "I have to get him adopted."

"First and foremost, exercise," Picote said. "Then, he should be socialized often and it would be best if he went to a home where he isn't alone very much. It's a bit of a dichotomy because he needs a calm environment, but at the same time, he needs to be intellectually challenged."

"What does that look like?" I asked. "It sounds like more than a brisk morning walk."

"It can be—don't underestimate a good walk to help calm a dog. But I was thinking along the lines of dog sports, although we really don't have anything like that up here in Northern Arizona."

I really didn't have time for it anyway. Between trying to solve Mario's murder and digesting everything my father had told me, as well as my nail business and the book I needed to write, taking Zeus to participate in dog sports was far down on my list.

Besides, a walk would be good for me as well and would get me out of my thoughts.

"There are some drugs we can try," Picote suggested.

I shook my head. "No. Not a fan of drugs." Especially after my dad's visit. So much so, I was willing to promise myself I'd never take another ibuprofen again. I'd get on board with Annabelle's herbal formulas. "But I'll keep that in mind if I can't exercise him enough."

"You have a yard, right?" Picote asked.

"Yes."

"You could set up a little homemade agility course to see how he does."

"That's an idea," I murmured. Hammer and Nail Hardware always had sales on planks of wood, and I could jerry-rig the rest.

"Anything else, Gina?"

"No, that's it."

"Do you want me to take a look at him? Run some blood tests?"

I mentally went over my schedule, trying to figure out where I could slip in a drive to Sedona and a vet visit, and there was no time. "I'll bring him in when I find someone to adopt him, just to make sure he gets a clean bill of health. I think that will be a while though, because I have to figure him out."

"Perfect. I'll see you then."

"Thanks for the phone call."

"Anytime. Good luck."

I set the phone down on the floor next to me and met Daisy's gaze. "What?"

"I heard 'walk.' I want to go on one."

"What if we need to take Zeus with us? It will make him nicer to be around."

Her gaze shifted to him. "I suppose so. Will it make him stop destroying things?"

I shrugged. "Maybe?"

"Okay, fine, he can go."

With great effort, I pushed Zeus off my lap and went to the laundry room to fetch the leashes. I really wanted to crawl into bed and sleep for two days, but that wouldn't be happening any time soon.

After getting the dogs ready, we headed out. I allowed them to stop and sniff where they wanted, sometimes spending long minutes waiting and hoping it would drain Zeus's endless energy reserves.

A mile into our walk, my phone rang. Trevor.

"Hey," I greeted him. "How are things going?"

"Are you busy tomorrow?"

I glanced at the dogs. "I have to walk the pups in the morning and then get some writing done and figure out how to build an agility course for my rescue. What's up?"

"Ah, as usual, you don't have a lot going on," Trevor said, chuckling. "I spoke to Billy Hoffman."

Billy Hoffman. Billy Hoffman. Who was he again?

"The guy Mario almost killed... the crime sent him to prison."

"Oh! Right! What did he say?"

His work radio sounded in the background. He cursed and told me to hang on. A moment later, he returned to the call. "I've got to go, Gina. There are cows loose out by the Tupper farm again. They need my help. I'll stop by in the morning."

CHAPTER 15

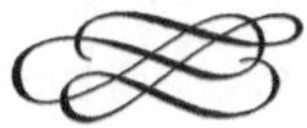

TREVOR DID SHOW up the next morning just after I returned from walking the dogs. He carried a tray with two coffees and a brown bag with the logo Cup of Go. I eyed the bag. Donuts? Scones? Muffins? It didn't matter. Everything from the coffee shop was delicious.

"Trevor! Trevor!" Daisy yelled as she jumped around him. "Hi, Trevor!"

Zeus pushed her out of the way to try to win over Trevor's attention.

"Knock it off, you jerk!" Daisy yelled, trying to retaliate by bumping him back and failing miserably. The Golden couldn't be moved by my forty-pound girl.

While Trevor scratched Zeus's head, Daisy slunk over to me and sat behind my legs. "I hate him," she pouted. "Trevor is my friend, not his."

I sighed but didn't answer. For Daisy's mental health and well-being, as well as my own sanity, Zeus needed to be adopted despite everything going well the past twenty-four hours. To my astonishment, he'd slept through the night without destroying any-thing, and had been perfectly well-behaved during our morning walk. The dog needed his exercise and mental stimulation of sniffing everything in sight, just as Dr. Picote had suggested.

"How are things going?" Trevor asked.

I shrugged, my heart and soul heavy. "Fine, I guess. My dad came to see me yesterday."

"How is he?"

I hadn't planned on telling Trevor every-thing my father had shared, but before I knew it, the whole ugly story came gushing out of me, the words bursting forth as fast as an active firehose.

Trevor simply stared, his hands on his hips and the dogs forgotten. When I finished, he pursed his lips and shook his head. "I... I wasn't quite expecting that."

"I didn't expect to share it with you."

"Should we have some coffee?" he asked, gesturing to the cups on the entry table.

"Sure." I led him into the kitchen, somewhat relieved after spewing my drama.

As we sat down, the dogs settled under the table.

"Zeus seems good today," Trevor noted.

I nodded and opened the bag. Raspberry scones. As my mouth began to water, I pulled one out and took a large bite.

"So good," I moaned.

"Yes, it is."

We ate in silence for a few minutes, then Trevor asked, "What are you going to do?"

"About the investigation?" I asked.

He nodded and took a sip of his coffee. "Are you going to follow his suggestion?"

"I'm not sure about that," I murmured. "I mean, he has zero proof Handlebar's the killer. He's able to connect him to Mario, but so were we."

"If he's right, you could be biting off more than you can chew, Gina."

"You're right. I don't want to get mixed up in that life."

"So maybe you should back off and leave it to the professionals."

I sipped my coffee while I considered my dilemma. "I can't do that to Sally, though. I promised her I'd help find the real killer. If we had a decent sheriff who wasn't willing to railroad everyone, then maybe I'd take your advice."

"Touché," he replied. "But I know Sally didn't do it, so let me handle the investigation. I'd feel horrible if something happened to you, Gina."

"Me too," Daisy said from under the table. "But I won't let anything bad happen. I'll protect you."

I didn't exactly have the biggest, bravest dog, so her words didn't hold much water.

"Honestly, I don't think Handlebar's involved," I said. "But I'll call Vic and see what he has to say."

"What about your mom?" he asked. "Are you going to look for her?"

"I don't know," I said. The idea had kept me up for hours in the night. "A lot of years have passed. She could've contacted me if she really wanted to see me. That leads me to believe she doesn't. Or, she could be dead."

"She could be thinking the same thing about you," he said softly. "Not that you're dead, but it's been so long, maybe you don't want to see the woman who abandoned you."

I hadn't thought of that. Even if I put myself in her shoes, I couldn't imagine anything keeping me away from my child, including my own safety.

I'd crawl to the other end of the Earth if it meant I was protecting Jacob. Was that the case with my mom? Had my dad lied about why she left? More questions for me to ponder. Just what I needed.

We finished our scones and coffee. "Do you want to hear about Billy Hoffman?" Trevor asked.

"Oh! I totally forgot about that," I exclaimed. My own issues had overshadowed his news. "Yes! Tell me!"

"Well, I called him on the phone yesterday to feel him out and ask him about Mario... or Peter. Billy knew him by Peter."

"What did he have to say?"

"The night that Mario almost beat him to death, they were at a bar. Both were drunk. Billy couldn't even remember what the fight was about. He woke up in the hospital two days later and the police asked if he wanted to press charges. He said yes. As we know, Mario went to prison for assault."

"Did you ask why he moved up here?"

"Said his parents live up this way, so that's why he came."

"So maybe sending Mario to prison wasn't enough revenge," I suggested. "Maybe he needed him dead."

Trevor shook his head. "No. Billy told me

he was in a car accident about two months ago. He's in a wheelchair."

"Maybe he's lying about that so you don't investigate him further."

"The same thing occurred to me, so I checked." Trevor said. "I called the Flagstaff police and they had a record of the accident. Billy had been drunk and plowed himself into a tree while speeding around a bend in the middle of the night. They needed the jaws of life to pry him out of the car."

I shrugged. "So what? People in wheelchairs are perfectly capable of murder."

"Of course, but in this case, I don't think it works. Billy said he's lost almost full function on his right side. His parents take care of him now. If he wanted to kill Mario, he'd have done so with a gun. There was too much destruction in that restaurant and the combat was hand-to-hand. It wasn't Billy."

"Well, at least we were able to rule him out," I said, somewhat disappointed. I spun my empty coffee container in my hand.

"Yes, that's the way I'm looking at it," Trevor replied. "I also checked our records. There hasn't been a sexual assault reported in Heywood in a long time."

It didn't really mean anything. Sexual assault went unreported a lot. Or maybe

Whitney was having an affair? But if so, that attraction had to be pretty strong for her to jump in the sack so quickly after meeting him.

After slipping off my glasses, I closed my eyes and rubbed my temples. Everything seemed so dark in my life. Although I was trying to not let it get to me, I couldn't tear my thoughts away from the fact my mother may be alive and the way my father had lied to me for so long. The betrayal ran deep, slashing at my insides like a knife. Should I look for her? Did she think about me at all? Or had she passed?

"Do you want me to do a search for your mom?" Trevor asked. "I can check the databases I have access to and see what I can find."

I glanced up at him and smiled. "You're sweet. Thanks. I'd appreciate that." But did I really want to go down that road? I wasn't sure. "If you find something, please don't tell me about it, though, okay? I have to think about whether or not I want this information."

"Why is that?"

"I'm just not sure if I want to poke that hornet's nest."

"You just want to get the stick ready in case you decide to move forward?" he asked, smiling.

"Something like that."

Trevor glanced at his phone, then back to

me. "Listen, I have about an hour before I need to be in the office. "So let's get busy and get this agility course built."

I furrowed my brow. "What?"

"You said you needed to build an agility course for Zeus, so I brought some stuff with me." He stood and motioned me to follow. "I've got it all in my truck."

Tears sprang to my eyes as I trailed him outside. Gosh, I hated crying, but my gratitude overwhelmed me. With the news about my mother, I felt small and vulnerable. The fact someone had taken a passing conversation and made it a reality just about did me in. "Trevor, I didn't ask you to do that."

"I know," he said. "But I thought it would be fun to build and that's what friends do... they help each other, right?"

He smiled as I examined the back of his truck—boards, bricks and some large plastic tubes big enough for Zeus to run through.

"I looked up how to DIY it last night," he said. "Let's get to work. This should be fun!"

I grabbed a tube and a couple of boards. Daisy followed me into the backyard. "Just to be clear, I'm not a circus dog," she said. "I'm *not* participating in this. This is for bad dogs, like Zeus."

"Right," I whispered under my breath. "Whatever you say."

"Maybe we should only put up a couple of things," I said. "We don't know how he's going to like this."

"That's a good idea."

We put up the plastic tunnel and built a jump out of bricks and a board. I hurried inside to fetch some high-value treats while Zeus studied everything carefully.

"I have no idea what I'm doing," I said. "I guess we should start with him sitting and going from there."

Daisy watched from the small patio.

"Sit!" I commanded the Golden, and to my surprise, he obeyed. I gave him a treat. "Stay!"

As he wagged his tail, I hurried to the other side of the jump.

"Come!" I yelled. He ran towards the jump, flew over it and kept coming. When I realized what his plan was, it was too late. He crashed into my legs and sent me sprawling into the grass. Both Daisy and Trevor laughed hysterically while Zeus tried to get the treats out of my hand and pocket. I rolled around as he pounced on top of me.

After a minute, I threw a few treats away from me and he hurried over to get them.

Quickly, I stood and brushed grass off my jeans.

Trevor strode over, his hands in his pants pocket, grinning. "I think he's got some work to do."

"I think you're right," I replied, laughing, my heart feeling lighter than it had in days. "But it's a start."

CHAPTER 16

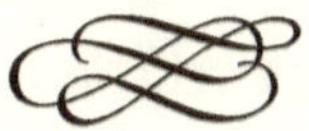

"Does he ever shut up, Gina?" Daisy groaned, her voice laced with sleep.

I sat up in bed, ready to strangle the Golden, and grabbed my phone. 3:45am. And he was barking in the living room as if Satan himself had just entered the house.

With a curse, I slipped on my glasses, threw back the covers and marched down the hall, ready to give Zeus a piece of my mind. I found him at the front door, his front paws up against it as he barked and snarled... like there was someone outside.

My breath caught in my throat as fear stiffened my spine. "Who's out there?" I whispered, slowly approaching him.

He continued his cacophony and I hurried to the front window. Just as I peeked through the blinds, I heard a motorcycle. It wasn't directly in front of my house, but down the street a bit. Recalling my immediate neighbors, I knew of a couple who owned bikes. But why was Zeus so upset?

The street was dark, as were the surrounding houses. Yet, I felt a presence outside. I glanced at Zeus, who had quieted, but still paced in front of the door.

I debated whether to go out. Something was off, that was for sure. Zeus was giving off all sorts of warnings, and I felt it in my bones.

"Maybe I should go back to bed and check out everything in the morning," I whispered.

Zeus whined, then sat down facing the door.

"What is going on out here?" Daisy said, trotting down the hall. "It's the middle of the night! Don't you know you aren't supposed to bark in the middle of the night unless it's an emergency, you big dork?"

And that was the problem. Since Zeus had arrived, he'd been silent at night, even when he was busy destroying something. There was definitely an issue in my front yard.

I hurried back to the bedroom and looked out the window there, which also faced the street. I couldn't see anything or anyone.

I debated returning to bed again, but I

knew I wouldn't be able to sleep. I'd never be able to doze off. Should I call the police? And tell them what? That I had a rescue dog who barked in the middle of the night and I had a bad feeling about the situation?

No, that wouldn't fly. I had nothing to report. No one was skulking around my yard. There wasn't any threat. I glanced out my window once again, the feeling that something was off growing stronger.

"I should check it out," I mumbled.

Was it smart for me to go out in the dark? Probably not, but I pulled on an oversized sweatshirt over my t-shirt and sweatpants anyway, then retrieved my revolver from the nightstand and slipped it into my pocket. After shoving my feet into a pair of sneakers, I leashed up the dogs.

"Don't make me go out there," Daisy whined. "It's dark. I don't like the dark unless I'm cozy in bed."

"Come on," I said. "If you see something or someone, just let me know."

"Zeus can do that," she pouted. "I just want to go back to the blankets, Gina. I don't like the dark."

"I can't have a conversation with Zeus," I countered. "I need you to come with me and use your super sniffer. If someone is out there, then I need to know who it is."

"You mean you need to know who it *was*," Daisy said. "Zeus says they aren't there anymore."

I nodded and a sigh of relief escaped me. "That's good to know. Let's go check things out."

"Okay," Daisy said, her mood suddenly shifting. "We'll be like the three musketeers!"

After flipping the lock and opening the door, I held the leashes in one hand and my gun in the other. Thankfully, no one met me on my front porch as I stepped outside. Glancing to my left, I didn't see anyone hiding in the corner shadows. I studied the front yard. Nothing. My driveway also stood empty, except for my car. The dogs both had their noses to the ground as I slowly walked toward the vehicle to examine it.

"Do you smell anything?" I whispered, wishing I'd had the wherewithal to bring out my flashlight.

"There was a bunny," Daisy said. "He peed right here."

I glanced down to see her in the grass. "I'm not worried about bunnies," I hissed. "Do you smell a human? A fresh scent?"

"Not around here."

I circled the car slowly, examining it for damage. Nothing stood out and no one attempted to grab me.

My shoulders slumped in relief. Zeus must've been mistaken, or someone was wandering around the neighborhood. All looked well at my house.

"Ask him what he was barking at," I instructed Daisy.

She stared at him a long moment as they had their doggy conversation. "He says there was someone out here. Then he also said, 'trucks, ducks and mice.' I don't know what that means. It must be his brain misfiring."

I glanced out at the street again as a chill traveled down my spine. "Maybe someone was out walking," I said. "I don't think anyone was at the house."

"Um... I don't know about that, Gina," Daisy said. "What does this mean?"

I turned to her. "What?"

"There. On the garage door."

Stay Away had been spray-painted across the white surface in black paint. How in the world had I missed that? I'd been so focused on the car and the street, I hadn't noticed the vandalism. Some sleuth I was.

I swallowed past the emotions swirling within me. Fisting my hands at my sides, I barely refrained from slamming one onto the top of my car.

After searching the neighborhood one last time, I marched back into the house with the dogs. I unclipped them from the leashes, then paced my living room.

Only one person could be responsible for the message: Handlebar. My father had said he might come for me since I was sticking my nose in his business.

"It has to be him," I said, then I turned to Daisy, who sat by the television watching me. "You didn't smell anyone different out there? Do you know Handlebar's scent?"

"I don't remember it," she said, lowering her head. "Sorry, Gina."

Dang it. "But you must've smelled someone out there, right?"

"Yes. But I didn't recognize the scent. It could've been Handlebar, but I don't know."

I continued to pace, muttering curses under my breath as my fury built. Now I'd have to fork over some money and have my garage door repainted and I wasn't going back to sleep for the night. I wasn't sure which angered me more. On top of that, how *dare* Handlebar threaten me?

This only made him more guilty in my book. He didn't want to be caught for murder, and he couldn't care less if someone else was put away for it. If he kept me out of the investigation and the sheriff was able to railroad Sally, then he was in the clear. He just had to be certain that I felt threatened enough to stay away.

He obviously didn't know me well.

"I need to talk to Vic," I said, pulling out my phone from my sweatpants pocket. Even though it was just after four in the morning, I dialed. He usually woke at five, so I wasn't being completely terrible.

"Gina?" he answered groggily. "What the heck?"

"Handlebar was just here," I said. "And he spray-painted my house."

After a moment of silence, he said, "What? Can you say that again?"

"Handlebar was here, Vic," I said. "Dad told me he may come for me because I was trying to figure out who killed Mario and that you getting out of the drug trade didn't really offer me protection any longer."

"He spray-painted your house?"

"Yes. It says, *stay away*."

"Stay away from what?"

"From the investigation!" I yelled. "Come on, Vic! Pull your head out of your butt and *think*!"

"Yeah, Vic!" Daisy shouted. "Pull your

head out of your butt!" She then dissolved into a fit of giggles.

"Look, I'm coming over right now," he ground out.

I almost told him there was no reason to unless he was going to match the paint and clean up my garage door, but I realized I liked the idea of having company. "Okay," I said. "I'll put on a pot of coffee." After hanging up, I went to the kitchen. Zeus barked at the back door, which sent my stress levels through the roof once again. I peeked out the window, but didn't find anyone or anything out of order. Once I opened the door, he ran outside. I quickly made the pot of coffee, then checked on him. Although the kitchen lights barely illuminated the yard, I found him trotting across the bridge Trevor and I had made, then he moved to the jump. After a quick bathroom break, he sniffed around the tunnel.

"He's interested in the agility course," I said.

"That's because he's dumb," Daisy retorted. "I could do that with my eyes closed."

"Then why don't you get out there?" I asked.

"Because I don't like the idiot. The more room between him and me, the happier I am."

I poured myself a mug of coffee and sat

down at the kitchen table. Caffeine was probably not the best thing for my nerves, but I sipped greedily. If I was going to get through this day, I'd need all the help I could get.

When a knock sounded at the front door, I hurried to open it. Vic walked in smiling, wearing a black cowboy hat and matching boots, a long-sleeved t-shirt and jeans with a button-down flannel shirt. "I smell the coffee."

"Then get in there and pour yourself a cup," I muttered.

Once we'd settled in at the table, he removed his hat. "Can you tell me from the beginning what happened?"

"You saw the garage, right?" I said.

"Yes. Did you call your cop friend yet?"

"No, I haven't."

"You may want to do that so there is a report of the incident," he said.

"I want Handlebar to go to jail for this."

Vic shook his head. "I'm trying to figure out why you think it's Handlebar."

"I told you why," I replied. "And I'm also angry you never told me about Mom, but we can hash that out later."

Vic sighed and raked a hand through his black hair. "Wow. Okay, so the old man really laid it all out for you, huh?"

"Yes, but like I said, we'll deal with that

later." I told him my story of Zeus waking me with his barking, of me leashing the dogs to head outside and then finding the spray paint. "Handlebar is warning me away," I said.

Vic pursed his lips and glanced around the kitchen. "That could've been anyone, Gina."

"Don't forget the motorcycle sounds we heard," Daisy said. "Tell him about that, Gina. Doesn't Handlebar drive a motorcycle?"

"Yes!" I shouted. I'd completely forgotten about that.

"Yes, what?" Vic asked.

"There was a motorcycle here," I blurted. "I heard it just before I went outside."

"Do you know how many people drive bikes around here?" Vic asked.

"But there's only one person who drives a motorcycle around here who would want to threaten me," I said. "And that's Handlebar."

With a satisfied smile, I picked up my coffee cup and took a sip.

"I don't know," Gina," Vic mumbled. "I don't think it's Handlebar who spray-painted your garage."

"There's no one else that it could be!" I yelled. "Quit protecting your stupid friend!" I stood and paced the small space. "I want to talk to him! Give me his number! I have a few choice words for that jerk, and I'm going to make him paint my garage himself!"

"No."

"Why not? Is he afraid of little old me?"

Vic chuckled and shook his head. "I highly doubt that."

"Then what's the problem?" I asked, spreading my arms wide.

"Handlebar is in jail right now," Vic said. "He was arrested for drunk driving. There's no way he could've been at your house tonight."

My bluster deflated quickly. If it hadn't been Handlebar, then who?

CHAPTER 17

Vɪᴄ ʟᴇꜰᴛ ᴊᴜꜱᴛ before the sun rose. I stood at the living room window, watching my neighbors as they discovered the graffiti on my garage. A couple whispered among themselves while pointing at my house. None of them actually came over to check on me, which was par for the course. Mr. Anderson, the cranky, elderly neighbor who hated dogs on his lawn, simply shook his head and shuffled back inside his house. The family who had moved in next door hurried to their car and drove away. I doubted any of them had even noticed. They were always off to one of the kids' school or sports functions and seemed to always be running late.

I sighed and shut the blinds, debating whether I should attempt to paint over the mess myself, or just hire someone to do it. Matching paint was not in my skill set, and I'd most likely end up with a bigger disaster than I already had.

Instead, I went outside with Zeus and worked the agility course with him. There were some failures, but he seemed to enjoy learning and the new challenges. The more I thought about it, I wondered if he'd be happiest as some sort of working dog. With plenty of farms around the area, maybe he could be trained to herd? He definitely needed a place where he was engaged mentally and got plenty of physical exercise.

I just wasn't quite sure what that perfect spot for him would be.

After our training session, I went inside and tried to avoid the feeling of defeat that seemed to settle around me. I'd been so certain Handlebar had been responsible for the threat because all evidence pointed to him, but Vic had assured me that wasn't the case. Reporting seemed like a waste of time, but I promised Vic I would.

I dialed Trevor directly. No way was I taking a chance of possibly dealing with Mallory if I called the non-emergency line.

"Someone graffitied my house last night," I

said. "It's a threat, and I want to make a report."

"A threat?" he replied. "What does it say?"

"Stay away."

A long beat of silence ensued. "Stay away? Are you thinking they're warning you away from the investigation, or have you gotten yourself into something else I don't know about?"

"Definitely the investigation."

"Do you feel you're in danger?"

"No," I sighed. "I didn't even want to phone, but I promised Vic I would."

"Okay. Let me get someone out there. I'm actually out on a call right now, so I can't come myself."

"Can we just do it later?" I asked. "The graffiti isn't going anywhere and I've got to get out of this house for a bit."

"Fine, but be careful, Gina. I don't like this new development one bit."

"I will," I muttered. "I'm not too happy with it, either."

After hanging up, I took a shower and decided to go into Heywood. As far as I knew, Trevor hadn't talked to Chris Raves at Too Hot To Handle, the hot sauce joint next to On The River. According to Trevor, Chris had cameras. Maybe he'd allow me to look at the footage if I asked nicely and bought a bottle or two of his Hell on Earth hot sauce I liked over my eggs.

"Can I please come?" Daisy asked as I ran a brush through my hair.

"Sorry, but not this time," I replied. "Chris doesn't like dogs in his store."

"I'll be a good girl and wait outside," she said hopefully, and I considered that for a minute. But, I had no idea how long I'd be in the store, and I'd only worry about her being tethered outside. Bringing her would only be a distraction to me.

"Daisy, if it were up to me, every business would allow dogs inside, and they'd have treats and a water bowl for their four-legged shoppers. But I don't rule the world."

"You should," she pouted. "Dogs should be allowed everywhere."

Ruling the world would probably be a little too big of a job for me, but maybe I could handle ruling Heywood.

Nope.

I had exactly zero patience for politics. Maybe even less than zero.

"I'm going to go," I said. Leaning over, I gave her a quick scratch.

"What are you going to do with Mr. Scrambled Brains?" Daisy asked. Unfortunately, I knew exactly who she was referring to.

"He seems pretty tired. Do you think we can trust him to just sleep on the couch?"

"Maybe, but I'd like you to lock me in this bedroom, please. I don't want his stink on our bed." I had a feeling she may also be a little afraid of him, which was understandable. He outweighed her by almost fifty pounds, and he'd proven himself to be somewhat untrustworthy.

"Done deal. I'll see if I can get him in the laundry room and I'll be back in a bit." I closed the door, then walked down the hall where I found Zeus stretched out on the couch, his tail thumping lazily against the cushions. After attempting to pull him off to put him in the laundry room and he didn't budge, I gave up. I didn't have the energy to wrestle the ninety-pound beast. "I'm leaving," I sighed. "Please don't destroy my house."

After he shut his eyes—which I took as a great sign that he'd mind his manners—I stepped outside and locked the front door. I hurried to my car, keeping my gaze averted from the warning, which I'd deal with later.

Traffic wasn't too heavy as I drove into town. I found a parking spot in the On The River lot, which didn't surprise me since the restaurant appeared to still be closed, but I did see Sally's car near the entrance. Maybe they'd released the crime scene and she was cleaning up? I'd stop by after my visit with Chris.

I hurried over to the store. As usual, he had plenty of business. A few locals and tourists all stood around listening to Chris' story about how he grew his own peppers. A friendly, charismatic man in his thirties, he held the full attention of his audience. I even found myself enthralled with the story I'd heard at least a half-dozen times.

When he finished, almost everyone lined up to buy something. I waited to the side, smiling hello at a couple of people I knew. The store had almost emptied when he walked over to me.

"Hey, Gina! Looking for some Hell on Earth?"

I nodded, impressed he remembered my favorite. "Probably a couple of bottles," I said. "I was also wondering if I could ask you some questions."

"Sure! What's up?"

"You have cameras out front," I said. "I was wondering if I could take a look at the footage from the night that guy was killed at On The River."

Chris grimaced and shook his head. "Terrible thing that happened over there. My cameras sure are a popular item in this town."

"What does that mean?"

"Well, you're the third, maybe fourth person that's been in here asking about them."

The hair on the back of my neck stood on end. "What do you mean? Who else was here?"

"Well, Trevor, who I think you know."

I nodded.

"Then Sally came over before the murder happened and asked me if they caught her place at all."

"Sally did? Why would she care?"

He shrugged. "She never told me why."

"Who else has been here?" I asked, still confused why Sally would want to know if her restaurant could be seen on Chris' cameras. A sinking feeling settled in my stomach. Was it because she had been planning to kill Mario and she wanted to be certain she wouldn't be caught leaving her establishment so late at night?

"I don't know his name," Chris replied. "Big guy showed up at closing the night of the murder and asked about them."

"Do you remember what he looked like?" I asked, my heart pounding. Even though Trevor said Handlebar was in jail, I couldn't shake the feeling he was responsible for Mario's death. If he was the one asking about the cameras, it would be just more proof he was guilty.

Chris shook his head. "It was dark. I'd just turned off the lights and he caught me off guard. I didn't ask any questions and I told him to hit the road and come back during business hours."

"And he left without an argument?"

"Yep." Chris chuckled, his white teeth seeming almost blinding against his dark skin. "I can sound pretty menacing when I put my mind to it."

I smiled, finding that hard to believe. "Do you still have the footage of that night?"

"Sure do. I made a copy for Trevor and decided it would be smart to keep the original for myself just in case."

"Would you mind if I took a look at it?" I asked.

"I suppose that would be okay. Come on back and I'll get it set up." I followed him behind the counter. "I'll be right with you, ma'am!" he called to a waiting customer.

The little office held a desk, chair, computer and a filing cabinet. Peppers hung from the ceiling, and a little worktable had been shoved into a corner. "Is that where all the magic happens?" I asked, pointing to it.

"Sometimes," he said. After firing up the computer, he sat down in front of it. "Most of the time, I make the sauce at home so I can be with the Mrs. and the baby."

"How are they doing?" I asked.

"Great. Man, do I like being a dad."

I used to wish I'd heard Jacob's father say something similar, but he'd been more interested in drugs, booze and other women.

"Here you go," Chris said, standing. "I've got to get out front."

As he hurried back to the store, I sat down, not exactly sure how to watch the footage. I moved the mouse around a bit, then finally found the "play" icon. Glancing at the time stamp and the lighting on the screen, I noted that I was watching the happenings around dinnertime.

The first thing that caught my attention was the number of motorcycles on the street and driving in and out of Sally's parking lot. I hadn't noticed this before, but I guessed I hadn't really been searching for them either. It made sense. Fall in the Arizona mountains offered beautiful scenery, and the temperatures were pleasant. It was perfect riding weather.

As I squinted at the screen, I didn't recognize anyone in the grainy footage.

Someone walked out of the back door at On The River and placed a bag of trash in the dumpster. Based on the build, it was definitely a man. Then, a while later, a woman stepped out and lit a cigarette. Sally didn't smoke, so it had to be one of her employees. When a motorcycle pulled up at the back door, I assumed it was Handlebar since Sally's server, Ginny Winn, had seen him bring in the drugs and argue with Mario.

I fast-forwarded to after dark. As the cars and motorcycles sped in and out of parking lot, I put the controller back to regular speed.

The parking lot was empty, except for Sally's car. And that car never left. It stood in the same place until the sun started to rise. The only other movement was a motorcycle that arrived, but quickly drove just out of the frame. I kept my eye on the doors to the building, but I never saw whoever that was enter or leave, and them driving away was never recorded, either.

I must have rewound and watched the video a dozen times.

Where in the world had that person gone? Maybe they'd pulled into the restaurant parking lot, then realized it was closed and left to go somewhere else?

Sitting back in the chair, I pulled off my glasses and rubbed my eyes, still tired from the pre-dawn shenanigans at my house. My brain was a little fuzzy, but I had the distinct feeling I was on the cusp of discovering who'd killed Mario... or maybe it was wishful thinking.

The video had left me with more questions than answers. I watched it one more time and realized I wasn't sure if I still believed Sally was innocent or not. But I also had a hard time believing she'd spray paint my house. Besides, I'd heard a motorcycle before I'd gone outside, and she didn't own one. But maybe that had been a neighbor? It hadn't been right outside my house, but down the street a bit.

Time to talk to her again and find out why she'd lied about leaving her restaurant that night.

CHAPTER 18

MY FEET FELT heavy as I walked over to On The River. I really didn't want to confront my friend, but at the same time, I had to get to the bottom of this. Maybe there was a simple explanation as to why she'd never left the building that night.

Or maybe she was a killer.

I had to find out.

After trying to push open the door, I found it locked. I rapped my knuckles on the window a few times and waited. Sally appeared a moment later.

"Gina! What are you doing here?"

"I was just over at Too Hot To Handle." I held up my bag of hot sauce and smiled. "I saw your car and thought I'd come by and see how things are going."

Sally glanced over her shoulder. "Everything is okay. I'm just cleaning up."

"Do you want some help?" I offered in the hopes that the conversation would flow naturally instead of me barging in and relentlessly accusing and questioning her.

She sighed and pushed her glasses up her nose. "That would be wonderful. Thank you."

When she stepped aside and I walked in, I noted the cleanup hadn't really begun—at least not in the main restaurant.

"I just finished tidying up the kitchen," Sally said, as if she'd read my mind. "And then I realized I was starving. I have enough ingredients for a couple breakfast burritos if you're interested."

My stomach growled on cue. "I've never been one to turn down a breakfast burrito."

"Come on back, then," she said. As we walked past the table where Mario had died, she pointed to the carpet. "I don't think that blood is going to come up. I'm wondering if I should even try, or just have it replaced."

Her statement caught me off guard. What a true, but odd, thing to say. A man had died in the space, and she was worried about the carpet? But then maybe that was her way of compartmentalizing the horror that had taken place. Instead of focusing on the loss of life, concentrate on what could be fixed to get her life back in order again.

I followed her into the kitchen where she picked up a knife and began chopping some bacon. The space was clean with everything in its place.

"Have you heard anything from the sheriff's office?" I asked, sitting on a stool across the table from her.

"Not really. I've talked to Mallory a couple of times and she's trying to trip up my story. Otherwise, they've been pretty quiet." She turned to the stove and expertly cracked a few eggs into a pan with one hand. Quite impressive. Then, she hurried to the refrigerator and retrieved two tortillas, laying each of them out on a blue plate.

Returning to the eggs, she moved them around the pan with a spatula while they crackled and snapped. Moments later, she pulled the pan off the flame and gently laid the eggs into the two tortillas. She did the same with the chopped bacon, and then grated some cheese into them. "This is my secret recipe," she said, giving me a wink as she picked up a silver can and shook it over the burritos. "It's the secret herbal blend that makes these so good."

I didn't dare ask her what ingredients

made up that blend. It was my understanding that every chef had their secrets that wouldn't be shared. Besides, I liked the idea of being kept in the dark about it because I'd certainly become frustrated beyond belief trying to replicate it.

She wrapped the burritos, laid them in a pan, then sprinkled more cheese on top, as well as more seasonings. "Have you found out anything about who killed Mario, Gina?" she asked as she set them into the oven and started the timer.

"Not really," I said, wishing I could eat the burrito before confronting her with her lie. "I've been asking questions, though."

She pulled up a stool and sat down across from me. "Who have you been talking to?"

"Well, oddly enough, Harry Dingle, or Hornet, came to see me," I said.

"Why would he do that?" she asked.

"Handlebar told him I wanted to talk with him, and he showed up at my doorstep, uninvited."

Her eyes widened and she shook her head. "What did he say?"

"In a nutshell, he didn't kill Mario, though he thought Handlebar could've done so." I shrugged. "He also alluded to the idea that he slept with Mario's wife, Whitney."

"Oh, my," she whispered. "I had no idea she was having an affair."

"I'm not a hundred percent sure it was consensual, but she never filed a report. It just seems a little off having just met someone and jumping into bed with them... unless, of course, she was getting revenge for her husbands' affair."

"Especially for someone her age," Sally said. "That bed-hopping is a young person's game." She shook her head and grimaced in disgust. "What else did he tell you? Was there anything that could lead you to believe he killed Mario?"

"Unfortunately, no. He got out of prison, came here to hang with Handlebar and his guys for a bit, and now he's gone to Michigan where he has family."

"Who else is there?" she asked.

"Well, the guy Mario almost killed, Billy Hoffman, we thought maybe he'd want revenge and he lives in this area over by Flagstaff."

"That sounds promising."

"I agree, except he's in a wheelchair and has limited movement. Trevor doesn't think he's physically capable of the violence done here."

The timer announced our breakfast burritos were ready. The beeping sound filled the air as she stared at me for a long moment. Finally, she said, "I'm not sure if I'm hungry now or not." She stood and fetched the burritos from the oven. After plating them, she set one down in front of each of us. Unfortunately, discussing murder had not slayed my appetite, so I picked up my fork and dug in. At least I could prolong my questioning until after I'd eaten the slice of heaven.

Sally watched me eat, but didn't touch her food. "I feel like you're crossing off suspects and my name still keeps landing at the top."

"That's not necessarily true," I lied. "Whitney could've killed her husband for the life insurance policy, and Mario kept telling his neighbor about all the money you had here."

"What was his name?"

"Danny Chavez," I said. I took another bite and groaned, loving it when the simplest things in life brought me such joy. "You said you were going to look for receipts to see if he'd been here."

"That's right," she said. "I got confused there for a moment. I did as you asked, and I found a receipt from the night of the murder for Andrew Daniel Chavez. I'm not sure if that's the same person, but that's the closest I found."

"And he was here the night Mario died?"

She nodded and finally picked up her fork.

"I think we have to assume that's the same

guy," I said, my leg bouncing with excitement. Maybe I didn't have to accuse Sally of murder. Perhaps Danny was only trying to provide for his young family. The economy stunk, and desperate people did desperate things, no matter what a good person they seemed to be.

He'd recently purchased a new truck, and Trevor was supposed to call Harry at Tinkering on Trucks to see if he'd sold any from his lot lately. Had he done that? If so, he hadn't mentioned it to me.

When my phone rang, I ignored it and allowed it to go to voicemail.

Sally wiped her mouth with a paper towel. "You think he was here casing the place after he'd heard how much money I kept around?"

"It sounds like a good possibility."

I finished the last of my burrito and decided it was time to confront my friend about her lie. "Sally, I saw footage from the night Mario was murdered." The words seemed to get caught in my throat and I began to cough. I took a few large gulps of water before saying, "You never left the restaurant."

"Of course I left," she replied. The grimace she wore told me she was offended by my accusation.

"Your car was there all night," I said, wishing I had approached this conversation with a little more tact. I didn't want to upset her, but I needed to get to the truth.

She burst out laughing, then shook her head. "Gina, after I fought with Mario, I was so upset, I walked home. Left through the door leading to the deck and took the Riverwalk up to the street."

"Oh," I said. I should have considered that. It also explained the motorcycle I saw in the footage. Maybe that person had also gone down to the Riverwalk, then entered through the deck?

As Sally ate, I stared at her, wondering if she was pulling the greatest scam of all time. She looked so innocent. I thought back to when my house had been vandalized. I'd heard a motorcycle, and I knew for a fact Sally didn't own one. It could've been a neighbor. My graffiti artist and the motor-cycle owner didn't have to be one and the same. "Did you hear what happened to my house?" I asked.

"No!"

While I shared the graffiti story, she stared at me with her mouth halfway open. "Oh, my gosh, Gina. How horrible!"

"I agree." I studied her face for signs she was lying. Instead, all I found was anger and disbelief.

"I can't believe someone would do that to you."

"Someone doesn't want me solving this murder."

"That's apparent," she replied with a small laugh.

"Is that you?" I asked.

Sally stared at me a long moment, then shook her head. "I suppose you needed to ask that. No, Gina. I swear on my mother's grave that I had nothing to do with Mario dying or the horrible defacing of your home." After standing, she took our plates to the sink and began rinsing them. She turned to me, angrier than I'd ever seen her in my life. As she planted her hands on her hips, her cheeks turned blood-red. "It wasn't me, Gina. And yes, I'm offended that you even asked, but it is what it is. If it's not me and it's not Billy Hoffman and Hornet has left town, that means there are two other people who could be responsible."

"Whitney or Danny?"

"Exactly," she huffed. "Now if you'll please leave, I have cleaning to do."

"I can stay and help you, Sally," I said softly, now regretting asking any questions.

"Thanks, but I don't want you here, Gina."

As tears welled in her eyes, I wondered, because of my lack of tact, if I'd just lost one of the few friends I had. Some people were capable of talking to others in a way that didn't come across as aggressive or accusatory. I was not one of those people.

I hurried through the kitchen to the front door, my phone once again ringing. After flipping the lock, I stepped outside and pulled the device out of my pocket. It was a number I didn't recognize.

The lock clicked behind me. Sally had completely shut me out. Would our relationship be repairable?

With a long sigh, I answered the phone. "Yes?"

"Gina?"

I pursed my lips and debated hanging up, but my gut feeling told me to stay on the call. "What?"

"My name's Lieutenant Hernandez from the Sedona Fire Department. Do you have a minute to talk?"

I tried to imagine what in the world he could possibly want and came up with a fat zero, unless my house had burned down. Glancing in that direction, I didn't notice any smoke. "Sure," I said, now curious.

"I got your number from Trevor Hutchison. He's a deputy there in Heywood."

"I know Trevor," I replied.

"Okay, good. Unfortunately, we just lost one of our search and rescue dogs to cancer," he continued.

"I'm really sorry to hear that," I said, still confused. "What does that have to do with me?"

"Well, although I know this sounds crass, we don't have the budget to buy a puppy. I was wondering if you knew of any rescues we may work with to train for the job? Preferably a high energy dog who loves activity and has shown that he or she is curious to learn?"

As I pursed my lips, my eyes welled. Holy moly. Had I just found a home for Zeus? "As a matter of fact, I think I have the perfect dog for you," I said. "He can be a jerk if he doesn't get enough exercise, but he's smart and likes to learn. He doesn't like to be alone, either."

"Oh, wow," he replied, chuckling. "He'll live at the station, so they'll always be someone around. He'll never be left alone. We'll also make sure he gets plenty of exercise. I'm so glad I called. When can I come meet him?"

CHAPTER 19

THE LIEUTENANT and I agreed to meet in the morning, and I tried really hard not to get my hopes up. Zeus could be an absolute jerk to the lieutenant and destroy his chances at adoption. I did feel it would be a good match, though. Zeus would never be left alone and he'd be busy. No lying around looking for something to destroy.

Not quite sure what to do with myself, I sat in my car and stared at the pavement in front of me for a long while, then decided to head over to Danny's place to ask him about his truck. He also owned a motorcycle, which ticked off a couple of boxes. First, according to the video I'd viewed at Too Hot To Handle, there'd been a motorcycle at Sally's place the night of the murder, but he'd come in and out of the line of sight so quickly, I hadn't been able to catch any details. Second, if that motorcycle I'd heard at my house in the early morning hours had belonged to my graffiti artist, it could've been Danny. Finally, he knew I was poking around into who killed Mario, so he'd definitely want me to "stay away" if he was guilty. And to top it all off, Daisy had smelled him at the restaurant and Sally had found a receipt for the night Mario was murdered.

Everything pointed to Danny as the killer, and I was in no mood to be nice to anyone any longer.

I swore under my breath as I headed home. If I was going to confront people, I would take my dog with me. Not that she offered any sort of real protection, but no one needed to know that.

After gathering her, I headed to Danny's house. Between being woken up so early, the warning spray-painted on my home, and me possibly losing one of the few friendships I had because I had such a hard time talking to people, my mood had sunk to beyond foul. Even the prospect of getting Zeus adopted did nothing to raise it because I was pretty sure he'd do something to ruin his chances. Maybe take a pee on the lieutenant's shoes or something equally vile. Nothing would surprise me with that one.

As I pulled up to the house, I saw the truck parked in the driveway. Where was the motorcycle?

I wasn't sure how to approach Danny, so instead of trying to finesse a nice conversation, I'd just say whatever came to mind. That usually didn't bode well for me, but whatever happened, happened.

"You stay here," I said, rolling down all the windows. "If I yell for you, start barking like you're big and mean and then jump out the window and run toward me. Snarl a little bit."

"So you want me to bring out my big, scary side."

"Exactly."

A low growl emanated from the back seat and I glanced in the rearview mirror. "How was that?" she asked, her tail thumping against the seat.

"Perfect. Remember, if I call your name, you come running."

"Okay! I can do that!"

I exited the car and marched up the driveway, my hands fisted at my sides. After knocking on the door, I crossed my arms over my chest and took some deep breaths. I probably should've called Trevor and asked him to come to this meeting, but it was too late now.

For some reason, I gasped when Danny's wife answered. Short in stature and round, she smiled and asked, "Can I help you?"

My balloon of fury began to deflate. I'd forgotten about her and the kids in my anger towards her husband. "Is Danny here?" I asked.

"No, he's not. Is there something I can do for you?" She tilted her head to the side. "I feel like I've seen you before."

"In your driveway," I replied, hitching my thumb over my shoulder. "I was talking to Danny when you and the kids drove up."

She snapped her fingers. "That's right. He said you were asking if he knew anything about that murder at On The River."

"Yes, I was."

"That's one of our favorite restaurants," she said. "But with the economy being so bad, we can't go out to dinner as much. It stretches our budget too thin."

"Hmm. Yes, I understand that. I really like your new truck, by the way. Did you buy it from Harry at Tinkering on Trucks?"

"Thank you. We went to Phoenix to get it. Unfortunately, it was cheaper down there than anything Harry had to offer."

She couldn't afford to go out to eat very

often, but they bought a new truck. "When did you get that?" I asked.

"Just a couple of days ago," she said. "We actually went down the day after the murder."

What perfect timing. Danny goes in, steals the money he's been hearing about from Mario, and Mario tries to stop him. Danny wins the fight, kills Mario and buys a truck the next day.

"I think your husband killed that chef," I blurted. "And I think I've got enough evidence to prove it."

Her round face turned ashen as her gaze widened in horror. "What are you talking about?!"

"I know you went to the church that night, and then you came home. You're going to say that your husband was with you all night, but can you actually be sure of that? Unless you stayed up until morning and never took your eyes off him, you can't be."

"You need to leave," she said. As she started to close the door, I put my foot out to block it. She stared at it a long moment, then narrowed her gaze on me. "If you don't allow me to close this door and you leave this property, I'll call the police and have you arrested for trespassing and harassment."

"Or maybe, we can just call the police and they can come arrest Danny," I suggested.

"He didn't do anything!" she yelled. "Danny would never kill anyone!"

"But he may have done it by accident for money."

She shook her head. "No. We live within our means. We budget our money. He's a man of God! Your claims are unfounded and ridiculous."

"A lot of women don't know their husbands," I said. "Trust me. I married the biggest jerk in town and didn't even really know until afterward."

Tears welled in her eyes, and a little bit of doubt settled into my gut. I was harassing the woman, and I really didn't have any proof of my claims. It was all circumstantial, but everything lined up perfectly. Yet, I suddenly felt pretty yucky about this situation.

A moment later, a motorcycle could be heard in the distance. I glanced over my shoulder to find it turning onto the street.

"That's Danny right there," his wife said. "You can tell him all this yourself."

He dismounted his bike and pulled off his helmet, then approached slowly. "What's going on?" he called.

Unfortunately, I didn't remember much of

my high school Spanish class, but I did recall a few choice curse words, which Danny's wife said again and again as she pointed at me.

"You seriously think I have something to do with Mario's death?" Danny asked as he ran his hand through his hair. "And now you're here harassing my wife?"

I was starting to feel a little bad about that, but I'd been threatened, and I needed to find the killer. "Where were you this morning?" I asked. "Say around four?"

He exchanged glances with his wife, then turned to me. "I was at work by four. They needed me to come in early, so I did."

"Call your boss and have him verify it," his wife ordered. "That way we can put this to rest and she'll leave us alone."

Maybe the wife was working with him? "And where were you?"

She swore again, this time in English. "I was home. I've got two kids with the flu. If you want to come in and help me wash the vomit-covered laundry, be my guest."

The three of us traded glances, and I was out of questions. I'd also run out of steam to throw around anymore accusations. In fact, I suddenly became bone tired.

I had no way to prove Danny had killed

Mario, nor could I ascertain he was at my house in the early hours of the morning.

"I think it's time for you to leave," Danny said quietly. "We didn't have anything to do with that man's death."

A motorcycle rumbled in the distance and based on the sound, it seemed to be going fast.

Mrs. Chavez rolled her eyes and swore again in Spanish while Danny let out an audible sigh.

As the bike reeled around the corner, I turned.

"Trouble has arrived," Danny said.

The motorcycle flew past the house and pulled into the next driveway—Whitney's home. As the big man dismounted the bike, he took off his helmet.

"Oh, my gosh!" I whispered. "What's he doing here?! He's supposed to be gone!"

"Gone?" Danny shook his head. "I wish. Since the day Mario died, that guy's been showing up here."

As Hornet sauntered up to the front door, I panicked. Was he a rapist? Should I go try to help Whitney?

But if that were the case, why would he keep coming back? Wouldn't she try to fight him off? Or was it one of those situations where she was beholden to her abuser for some reason?

Then I noted the *For Sale* sign in the front yard. For a second, it felt as if my brain had somehow short-circuited. I stared at the white sign featuring the man with overly white teeth. Since I knew him, I was fully aware his teeth were nowhere near that white, nor did he have that much hair.

But that was beside the point.

As all the puzzle pieces found their partners, I realized I'd finally discovered the killer.

CHAPTER 20

"I am so sorry," I muttered, turning to the couple. "I... that guy told me he was leaving the area."

Danny shook his head. "Nope. He's been hanging out at Whitney's house since the day Mario was killed."

"Okay," I whispered. "Now what do I do?"

"What do you mean?" Danny asked.

"I'm pretty sure he and Whitney murdered Mario. Or maybe he did it, but Whitney gave her blessing. Has she said anything recently to you?"

Mrs. Chavez nodded. "I saw her last night while getting my mail. She said she was going to Michigan, and if I could keep an eye on the house while it sold, she'd appreciate it."

So the whole hair model in Colorado plan

had changed. Or had it been an elaborate lie to hide her true intentions? "Did she say when she was leaving?"

"Either today or tomorrow," Mrs. Chavez said. "She claimed to have some loose ends she needed to tie up."

Of course she did. Things like making sure the life insurance company had an address to send the check to... and probably selling some drugs they'd gathered from On The River during the killing.

"That guy has been in and out at all hours," Mrs. Chavez continued. "When I was up with the kids last night, I heard him come and go at least three times."

And I was willing to bet, at least one of those times he was spray-painting my house. "What an absolute jerk."

"Both of them are," Danny sighed. "I wish they'd leave and let the rest of us live in peace."

"Why don't you two go back inside?" I suggested. "I'm going to call the police."

The husband and wife exchanged glances. "Do you think we should leave the neighborhood?" she asked.

I had no idea. Bullets may fly, or maybe I was simply wrong again. But, I'd rather be safe than sorry, especially when children were involved.

"Yeah, take those babies and head to On The River," I replied. "Tell Sally that Gina sent you, and then tell her that I'm getting to the bottom of it."

"Will she know what you mean?" Danny asked, his brow furrowing in confusion.

"She'll understand. Then tell her to call Annabelle over at Sage Advice and get your kids some of that ginger tea. It tastes awful, but it works wonders."

I didn't want Hornet or Whitney to see me, so once the Chavez's were inside, I walked around to the other side of the house, away from Whitney's, and phoned Trevor.

"Hey Gina," he said. "Did Lieutenant Hernandez call you? I thought maybe Zeus would be a—"

"Yes, but right now I need you to listen to me," I interrupted.

"Oh, no," he muttered. "What's up?"

"I know who killed Mario."

"Oh, really?"

"Yes."

"Is this a stab in the dark, or do you have concrete evidence?"

I didn't bother to share the fact that I'd already burned two bridges today with potential suspects. "The evidence is in Whitney's house," I said. "I know it."

"Gina, I need more than that to go busting into someone's home."

I pinched the bridge of my nose and sighed. "Okay, hear me out."

After explaining my theory and lining up all the evidence, Trevor was quiet for a long moment. "You need to stay away from there," he said.

"I'm already here, Trevor," I whispered. "Which means *you* need hightail it over here. *Now!*"

After hanging up, I stuffed the phone in my pocket and decided on my next move. Did I confront Whitney and Hornet, or did I wait for Trevor?

Sounds came from the front of the house and I moved to the edge where I could view the driveway. The Chavez family had heeded my suggestion and were loading in the car, the kids wrapped in blankets. Poor things. I hated to drag them out of bed or from a good episode of Paw Patrol—especially when they were sick—but if things got dicey around here, I didn't want them in danger.

I made a mental note to apologize again for my behavior to Mr. and Mrs. Chavez. Gosh, I could be a grade-A jerk when I was tired and irritated.

Mrs. Chavez stared at me as they drove

away. Was she worried about me? Or maybe she hoped Hornet would put a bullet into me after the way I'd spoken to her.

I stood at the corner of the house for a very long time. It hadn't seemed like Hornet had noticed me at the Chavez doorway, which was good. I had the element of surprise. But what did I do with it?

It seemed best to wait for Trevor and help him confront Whitney and Hornet, but when I heard a car start and a motorcycle rev, I stepped from my hiding spot to take a look. Whitney was in the car waiting for Hornet to back out of the driveway.

Dang it. It seemed if I didn't confront them now, we may never get the chance.

After taking a deep breath, I hurried into the street and stood at the end of the driveway. I noted the backseat of the car was packed with miscellaneous things, one of them being a laundry basket and a suitcase. They were leaving town.

Hornet stopped when he saw me in the rearview mirror, then turned around. When I lifted my chin and crossed my arms over my chest, he must have received the message that I wouldn't be going anywhere. He could drive around me, but Whitney would have to go over me to follow him. Hopefully, she had no plans to do so.

Hornet killed the engine and dismounted the bike while taking off his helmet. A small smile crossed his face as he approached. "Gina. What are you doing here?"

"I should be asking you the same thing," I said. "What happened to Michigan?"

"I'm on my way now."

Whitney exited the car and hurried toward us. "What's going on?"

"I'm not sure, babe," Hornet muttered. "But I think Gina here is about to tell us."

"Well, I'm stopping two killers from leaving the state," I said, studying both of their faces carefully.

Hornet threw his head back and laughed while Whitney's face paled.

"You don't have any proof of that," he scoffed. "Now, get out of the way."

I glared at Whitney. "I finally put it together," I said. "You told the police you had multiple pen pals at the prison, but you hit it off with Mario. You and Hornet here also grew close, right?"

She glanced from Hornet back to me, then shook her head. "I have no idea what you're talking about."

"Sure you do," I retorted. "Maybe you

couldn't decide which one you wanted the most—Hornet or Mario—so you played both of them. But then you and Hornet developed a deep connection." I turned my attention to the man in question. "You must write one heck of a love letter from prison."

His nostrils flared while he fisted his hands at his sides.

"When Mario said he was getting out and he had a life insurance policy, an idea started to form," I said. "Why not have Whitney marry him, then kill him off shortly after for the money? But then, he got you, Hornet, in trouble at the prison, so you had to stay longer, which only added to the reasons of wanting him dead. Money can be a powerful motivator, but combine that with a little revenge, and you've got a lot of reasons to kill him. As soon as you were out, the plan was put in motion."

Whitney gasped and placed her hand over her mouth. "What? I'm so confused!"

Where the heck was Trevor? I couldn't physically restrain both Whitney and Hornet and I didn't have my gun with me. It was two against one, and I didn't stand a chance.

"You're ridiculous," Hornet said. He smiled, but the vein in his neck was visibly pounding under the skin, letting me know I was most certainly on the right track.

"Am I, though?" I asked. "The drugs, not to mention the money Sally stored at the restaurant were just the icing on the cake. Poor Handlebar had no idea you'd take advantage of the fact that he was supplying Mario with drugs, and he *told* you about it." Pursing my lips together, I shook my head. "You get your revenge for Mario keeping you in prison longer, you got the drugs, Sally's money, and Mario's wife. You really cleaned up, Hornet."

"What have you done?" Whitney whispered, stepping away from Hornet. "What did you do to Mario?"

"Oh, give it a rest," I said, rolling my eyes. "The jig is up, Whitney. You're just as guilty as Hornet, if not more so. If I had to guess, you're the brains and he's the muscle."

Whitney narrowed her gaze as her jaw worked, finally dropping the innocent persona. "Get out of the way, Gina," she hissed. "I've been waiting too long for all this to come together. If you don't move, I'll move you myself."

"I'd like to see you try," I said. "I'm not leaving until the police come here and arrest you and lover boy here. Mario never had a chance with you, did he? From the start, as soon as you discovered he had a life insurance policy, your little hamster wheel went into high speed. I wouldn't be one bit surprised if your plan is to get rid of Hornet when you get to Michigan. You can't have two dead significant others in the same town, right? That would be a little bit obvious."

Whitney face contorted into something resembling rage and desperation. As she lunged at me, a primal scream rang through the air. I stepped aside before she could grab me. As she fell onto the pavement, Hornet grabbed me from behind, his arms a vise around me. No matter how hard I struggled, I couldn't break his grasp. "Daisy!" I yelled. "Daisy, now!"

I continued to fight while waiting for my dog to come to my rescue. Whitney rose, baring her teeth. She leapt toward me again. This time I leaned against Hornet, raised my feet, and smacked her in the stomach. As she doubled over, Hornet began dragging me toward the house.

"We're putting an end to this," he growled in my ear. "I'm going to shoot you in the house, then stuff you into one of the closets. They'll find you at some point."

That plan wasn't going to work for me, so I tried to reason with him. "If you do, the realtor will find me and he'll know Whitney had something to do with the death."

Hornet was now carrying me, my feet

barely scraping the driveway. As I struggled to pry his hand off me, I noticed for the first time that his fingernails were black... as if they'd been stained while spray painting. "Let go of me!" I yelled. "Daisy! Daisy!""

"Who the heck is Daisy?" Hornet muttered. "She won't be able to help you."

Suddenly, I heard growling and my attacker came to a halt. "What the..."

For a second, I thought my dog had finally come to my rescue, but the growl didn't sound like her. It was far too deep. Hornet swung me around toward the sound, putting me in between him and... a gray pit bull whose ears were plastered on his head and the scruff of his neck stood on end.

I knew most pit bulls were only mirrors of how their owners treated them, but I had to admit, this big guy scared me into silence.

"Maybe I should let this dog take you down," Hornet whispered in my ear. "Then it'll look like an accident."

The pittie growled again. Drool dripped from his chin, and I was more terrified than I'd ever been. My breath caught in my throat as I tried to scream, and I wasn't sure if I should fight against Hornet more or simply be still. Being mauled by a dog was not the way I wanted to go out, and this big canine seemed to be up for the job.

Where in the heck had he come from?

"Don't hurt her!" I recognized that voice.

To my left, Daisy came trotting around the corner. She stood next to the pittie and growled as well. They seemed to be... working together?

Both moved toward us. Hornet still had me placed between him and the dogs.

"Don't worry, Gina," Daisy said. "This is my new friend, Bruno. He belongs to the Chavez family and hates Whitney and Hornet. He told me they throw rocks at him over the fence. Isn't that mean?"

I relaxed a bit, feeling better that Bruno was on my side. Hornet didn't need to know that though.

"It's the neighbors' dog!" Whitney shouted from the bottom of the driveway. "Hornet, run!"

Hornet let me go. As my feet finally met the pavement, I turned to see Bruno and Daisy chasing the man, who was now running toward Whitney. Screaming at the top of her lungs, she hustled back to the car, got in and slammed the door. Hornet stood on the other side of the bike, as if that could protect him from Bruno and Daisy leaping over it. They had him pinned. If he ran, they'd attack him. If he stayed, the bike offered a bit of weak protection, and he seemed to realize this.

A moment later, Trevor arrived. He took in the scene with wide eyes, then yelled, "Call the dogs off, Gina!"

"Daisy, come!" I shouted. Bruno gave one last growl, then he and Daisy trotted up the driveway and sat at my feet. As I gave them scratches behind their ears, I whispered. "Thanks, guys."

"We were awesome, weren't we, Gina?" Daisy said, her tail wagging. "I knew I wasn't scary enough, but Bruno is!"

"How did you know about him?" I asked.

"While you were talking to those two people on the porch, I smelled him. We had a little talk through the side fence and he was able to open it and get out. Then, we waited by the car for you call for me! We saved the day!"

I chuckled as Trevor put the cuffs on Hornet and Whitney. Hornet stared at the ground in defeat, while Whitney cried. Were they tears of regret that she'd been caught, or regret for what she'd done? I had the feeling I knew the right answer. The woman was a dangerous grifter who deserved to be behind bars.

A moment later, a second sheriff's car arrived, and Trevor loaded Hornet into it, then put the sobbing Whitney in his.

"Are you okay?" he asked, approaching me slowly.

"I'm fine," I said.

"Good work putting it all together."

"Thanks. I'm just glad you didn't kick me out of the restaurant when you were interviewing Whitney, or I never would have known she had multiple prison pen pals. That, and the way she was acting in my store sealed the deal that she was involved."

Trevor nodded, placing his hands on his hips. "So where are you off to now?"

I thought about repairing my garage, but realized I had something far more important to tend to. "I have to go mend some bridges."

I LOADED the dogs into my car and headed to On The River. Both sat in the back seat with their tongues hanging out, obviously very proud of their accomplishment in helping me catch the bad guys.

Hopefully, me bringing Bruno back to the family would earn me some points and they wouldn't end up hating me too badly.

Once we arrived, I let the dogs out of the car and the three of us walked to the front door. After attempting to open it and finding it locked, I tapped my knuckles against it. A moment later, Sally answered.

"Are you okay?" she asked.

"Yes. Did the Chavez family come here?"

"They did. Come on in."

After I entered, I allow a moment for my

eyes to adjust. I hated the idea of sending these people to a place where evidence of a brutal murder had happened, but I knew they'd be safe there and Sally would take care of them.

Except, there wasn't any indication of any altercation now. The glass had been swept up, the tables righted. Those that had been broken were gone—most likely in the dumpster. As I walked through the restaurant, the only clue to the killing was the bloodstained carpet, and a table had been strategically placed there, so it was only visible to someone who was aware of it.

Sally led me into the kitchen where I found the Chavez family. The kids were tucked away in a corner on a makeshift bed of blankets, watching tablets. Bruno ran over to them, his tail wagging, and immediately burrowed in between them as they yelled his name and wrapped their arms around the big beast. He may appear mean, but it was obvious he loved his kids.

"What happened?" Danny said, standing from the stool he'd been sitting upon. Sally had made him and Mrs. Chavez coffee. "Are they gone?"

"They've been arrested," I said. "They didn't give a confession, but I have a feeling Whitney will break with even the slightest amount of pressure. I think she was the brains and Hornet was the brawn. She'll throw him under the bus."

"Thank goodness," Mrs. Chavez whispered, then made the sign of the cross. "Our neighborhood is safe again."

"Don't think she can stomach prison?" Sally asked.

I shook my head. "No way."

The three adults stared at me as heat crawled up my neck. I cleared my throat. "Look, I wanted to apologize," I began. "I said some pretty awful things and made some big accusations to all of you. I'm sorry."

"We were just talking about that," Sally said. "You weren't very nice, Gina."

"I know. I'm... I'm really tired and stressed out. My garage was spray-painted this morning, and it scared me to death. I was desperate to find who the killer was. I should've had more tact."

"Tact is not your strong suit," Sally mumbled.

"It's not," I admitted. "I hope you'll all accept my apologies."

Sally narrowed her gaze, then walked over to me and took me into a big bear hug. "I know you aren't a hugger," she whispered. "But you look like you need one. Relax and try to enjoy it."

I allowed the stress in my shoulders to fade and closed my eyes. It did feel nice to be cared for by someone. A moment later, she released me and smiled. "Now, you look like you need some coffee."

"I do."

"You're in luck," Sally said as she poured me a cup. "With fall being here, I've whipped up a little of my pumpkin spices and it just so happens, they taste amazing in coffee."

"They really do," Danny said. "I'm on my third cup."

"You'll never get to sleep tonight," Mrs. Chavez muttered as she shook her head.

"That may come in handy with the two barfers over there," he said, hitching his thumb over his shoulder.

Just then, Annabelle burst in through the back door where Handlebar had delivered the drugs. I wondered how long Mario had been dealing and how much product had moved out of the innocuous restaurant. I was sure Sally would do full background checks on anyone she hired to take his place.

"Here they are!" she said, holding up a paper bag. "These things, are like, the absolute best for upset tummies!" Today she wore a neon yellow tracksuit with pink tennis shoes. Bracelets jangled up and down her arms, and her eyeshadow matched her clothing. I noted a Duran Duran t-shirt poking out from beneath the jacket. "Gina! Are you okay?"

"I'm fine," I said. "Just tired."

"You're fine thanks to me and Bruno," Daisy said. "You never give me credit where it's due."

"I brought the kids some lozenges," she said. "I don't think they'd like the taste of ginger tea."

How anyone stomached it, I had no idea.

"You can give them each one every three hours," Annabelle said, handing the bag to Mrs. Chavez. "Make sure they get some electrolytes, and they should be feeling much better tomorrow."

"Thank you," the woman said. "How much do we owe you?"

"Oh, it's on the house," Annabelle said. "Any friend of Gina's is a friend of mine." She snorted and rolled her eyes. "Not like she has a ton of friends, but you know what I mean."

She wasn't wrong, but it still hurt a little.

Mrs. Chavez smiled, then looked at me. "I guess you coming into our lives wasn't the horrible thing I thought it to be."

I grinned while trying to decide whether to

be offended or not, and instead decided to head home. Everyone in the Chavez family was safe and they most likely wanted to get back to their house, too. "I'm taking off," I said. "My bed is calling my name."

"Thanks again for everything, Gina," Sally said. "Both Danny and I appreciate your efforts. Tomorrow afternoon is the grand re-opening of the restaurant, and I hope you'll come by."

"Yes," Danny said. "Thank you."

I waved over my shoulder as Daisy and I headed toward kitchen door, then out the side of the building. We walked up to the parking lot and entered the car. With a sigh, I leaned my head back against the headrest.

"Let's go home and see what that big dummy has done to the house," Daisy said. "I hate him."

"He may have a new home to go to," I said. "Keep your paws crossed."

"Who's taking him? When do you find out if he's leaving?"

"Tomorrow," I said. "It all happens tomorrow."

~

THE NEXT DAY, I woke early to walk Zeus, hoping the exercise would make him presentable to the lieutenant.

When we returned from the walk, I found Trevor in my driveway painting over the graffiti on my garage door.

"Why in the world would you do that for me?" I asked.

"Did you want to keep it?"

I laughed and shook my head. "No, but... but that's really nice of you, Trevor."

"What can I say? I'm just that type of guy." He held out a brush. "Care to join me?"

After tying Zeus to the porch and unleashing Daisy to allow her to sniff around the yard, I picked up a brush. "You matched the paint perfectly," I said, thoroughly surprised.

"Another one of my skills," he replied. "Catching bad guys and matching paint. I'm full of great attributes."

We painted in silence for a long while, and I found it surprisingly calming to see Hornet's message slowly disappear. Maybe he should've stayed away from me and then he wouldn't be back in prison.

"Just so you know, we found drugs and a bunch of cash in Whitney's car," Trevor said. "After the case is over, I'm going to see if Sally can get her money back because I'm sure some of what we found is hers."

"That's great!" I exclaimed. "She'll be so happy to hear that. Losing that much money would've been quite the financial blow."

"Agreed. And hopefully, she figures out another system to keep the cash instead of stowing it at the store overnight. Even if she got a floor safe or something, it would be better than her sticking it in the desk drawer."

Zeus started barking when a car pulled up to the curb. Trevor and I set down our paintbrushes when a man approached.

"Marko!" Trevor called as he crossed the lawn. "How's it going?"

"Daisy," I hissed and she trotted over. "Go tell Zeus this is his big chance. If this guy takes him, he's going to be living a great life with a lot of exercise and running through the mountains."

"Ugh," she said. "That sounds horrible. I like my bed and squeaky toys."

"Well, you aren't going," I muttered. "Go tell him to mind his manners."

She trotted over to the Golden and sat down in front of him. I smiled as the two men approached.

"Marko, this is my friend, Gina," Trevor

said. "Gina, this is Lieutenant Marko Hernandez."

"It's nice to meet you," I said. "Thanks for coming." Standing at just over six feet with salt and pepper hair, I placed him in his forties. The broadness in his shoulders and muscular torso told me he worked out religiously. I imagined with his job, he had to be in excellent physical shape.

"I've heard a lot about you," Marko said as he shook my hand. "What happened to the garage?"

What exactly had Trevor told him about me? I had to assume some of it was good, or he wouldn't be here helping me paint my garage.

"Gina got messed up in some bad business, and we're painting over the warning she was given," Trevor said.

"That's too bad." Marko's brow furrowed. "I hope you caught the guy responsible."

"We did," I said. "Are you ready to meet Zeus?"

"Heck, yes. Let's see the big guy."

I pointed to the porch where Zeus stood, his tail wagging.

"That's one big Golden," Marko said. "He looks strong."

"He is," I muttered.

"Hey, Zeus," he said as we approached. "Are you the guy I'm looking for?"

To my utter shock, the dog stayed seated. With his tongue hanging out and his tail swishing back and forth, he seemed like a sweet Golden retriever.

Marko held out his hand, and Zeus gave it a quick smell, then licked it. "What do you think, buddy? Are you smart enough to be on the search and rescue team? You know, we only take the best."

"He's not smart enough," Daisy said. "But please take him anyway."

"We set up an agility course in back for him if you want to take him there and see what he can do," Trevor suggested.

"Great idea," Marko said. "Let's do it."

As we went through the house to the back, I appreciated Trevor's help in getting Zeus rescued. I held on to a small sliver of hope that the dog would do exactly as I asked him.

I ran Zeus through the paces, and he kept running back to Marko, as if to say, "Did you see that? Did you see what I did?"

He did well, except he wouldn't come to me, even when I offered him a treat.

Marko gave him some basic commands, and Zeus obeyed to perfection.

"Now he's just being a showoff," Daisy muttered.

"That's okay," I whispered as I bent down to pet her. "We want him to be a showoff so Mark takes him."

"I can run that course just as fast as him, Gina. And I'm much better at sitting."

"Of course you are," I murmured.

About twenty minutes later, Marko came over to me with Zeus at his side. "I think he's got some potential, Gina."

My sliver of hope turned into a full piece. "Really?"

"Yes. I think with the right handler and training, he can be a big asset to us."

Tears sprang into my eyes. "So... you're going to take him?"

"I think I will," he said. Zeus jumped up and placed his front paws on Marko's shoulders, then licked his face. With a laugh, Marko rubbed behind his ears, then commanded the dog off. Zeus sat at his feet, staring up adoringly. "How much do I owe you, Gina?"

Relief crashed through me like a large wave on the seashore. I shook my head. "Nothing. He's a donation to the department."

"Really?"

"Yes. Just please let me know if he doesn't

work out. I can take him back and try to re-home him."

"You better be good, Zeus," Daisy yelled. "I don't want you around here anymore, so don't mess this up and come back! If you do, I'll make your life even more miserable! Do you understand me, you golden buffoon?"

"Will do, Gina," Marko said. "You ready to come with me, big guy?"

Zeus licked his hand, then we all walked back to the front yard. As the Golden and Marko loaded into the car, Trevor and I waved.

"I mean it, Zeus! Don't be a turd! I never want to see you again!" Daisy yelled.

After they drove away, calmness settled over me. The murderer had been caught. I'd found someone for the unruly Golden retriever. It seemed Sally had forgiven me, and the Chavezes wouldn't be taking out a restraining order. My life seemed to be back in order.

"Should we get back to the garage?" Trevor asked.

With a groan, I turned around to see the *Y* in *Away* still visible. "I'd forgotten about that."

"Let's finish it up and then I'll take you to lunch at Sally's," he said.

"Back to the scene of the crime, huh?"

"Yes. Back to the scene of the crime and the best food in Heywood."

I wanted to support my friend, but did I want to eat in the place where a man had been murdered? My stomach flipped at the thought, and I almost declined his invitation. Then I remembered my favorite menu item. "Do you think Sally will have breakfast burritos?"

"If not, I'm sure we can put in a request to the chef." Trevor chuckled. "I mean, you did solve a murder."

I smiled in agreement. Yes, I definitely deserved breakfast burritos.

But now I also had time to focus on my family, which left a pit in the middle of my soul.

Thoughts whirled in my head. What had really happened to my mother?

Was she alive?

If so, why hadn't she contacted me?

EPILOGUE

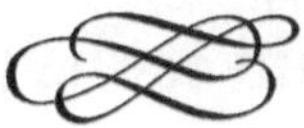

THE HOLIDAYS HAD PASSED, and I was sick and tired of being cold. As I turned up the heat in File It Away, I glanced out to see it was snowing yet again. Sure, we were in a drought, but enough was enough. At least I'd gotten to spend three weeks with my son, Jacob, who had come home from college. We'd watched all our favorite Christmas moves, had a big Christmas dinner with my father and brother, and Trevor also joined us. I'd also finished ghost-writing the mystery novel and turned it into the author. I had no idea what mystery my next book would tell, but I hoped no one else was murdered here in Heywood. Although it made my job as a writer much easier, I didn't want to be involved in any future investigations.

Yes, it had been a beautiful and productive holiday season, but everyone was back to their normal schedules now.

Except my dog.

"Daisy, you're going to have to go outside at some point," I said as she paced the length of the salon.

"I don't like my feet wet, and I don't like being cold," she muttered.

Considering she hadn't been out since the prior afternoon, I imagined her bladder was bursting at the seams. I worried about an infection. "Well, it's snowing again, so you better get out there sooner rather than later because the more snow there is, the wetter your feet around going to be and the colder you'll get."

She grumbled something while I pulled out my phone and glanced at my scheduling app. I swore when I realized my first appointment, Erika, was late. She worked as a checker at Hammer and Nail Hardware and absolutely loved to have her nails in top shape, mainly because she had a Tic Tok channel where she shared beauty secrets and makeup tutorials. According to Erika, one can't show someone how to apply eyeshadow with ugly, unkept nails.

Twenty minutes went by. My irritation

turned to worry. It was highly unlike her to not show. In the past if she was running even a few minutes late, she texted. I tapped my fingers against the counter while Daisy continued to pace.

I picked up my phone and sent her a quick text.

EVERYTHING OKAY? You're late for your nail appointment.

I STARED at the screen and waited for a reply. When there wasn't one, my worry only grew. It was even stranger for her not to answer my text. In her twenties, her phone was never more than a few inches away from her.

"Okay! Okay!" Daisy yelled, running for the door. "I can't hold it anymore!"

After grabbing the leash, I left a note taped to the door and Daisy and I walked up Comfort Road a few blocks. I wasn't happy about being out in the cold, either, but I kept my thoughts to myself. Maybe I could teach her to use the toilet?

"There was a bunny here," Daisy said while sniffing the base of a tree.

"Do you need to go to the bathroom again?" I huffed, irritated with her exploration.

"No. I'm done."

"Let's head back to the store."

When we arrived, Trevor stood at the door dressed in his sheriff's uniform and parka, a baseball hat and gloves.

"Hey," I greeted him. "What are you doing here?"

The grimace never left his face. "I need you to come with me."

"What's going on?" I asked. After unlocking the door, we both stepped inside.

"There's been a murder," he growled as he rubbed his hands together.

"Oh, no," I sighed while dread curled my stomach. "Who is it?"

"Molly Griffin."

"I don't know her," I said, furrowing my brow.

"Well, Erika Roscoe does, and she's down at the station."

"Erika?" I shrieked. "She's supposed to be here!"

"She's not going to be getting her nails done anytime soon," Trevor replied. "She says you're the only one she'll talk to about her friend's death, so like I said, I need you to come with me."

Why in the world did Erika want to speak with me about her friend's murder?

Find out in Fur Balls and Fatalities, available at your favorite retail outlet or direct from me at a discounted price.

ALSO BY CARLY WINTER

The Heywood Hounds Cozy Mysteries

(Humorous cozy mysteries featuring a talking dog)

Amateur sleuth, Gina, and her talking dog, Daisy, solve murders in the small town of Heywood, Arizona.

The Heywood Herbalist Cozy Mysteries

(Small town contemporary cozies)

From Hollywood, California, to Heywood, Arizona, trouble follows her...

After her husband's brutal killing and her fall from the Hollywood elite, the disgraced Samantha Rathbone moves to Heywood, Arizona, hoping to forget her past and live a quiet life of anonymity.

It doesn't go as planned.

Sedona Spirt Mysteries

(Paranormal cozies)

Bernie and the ghost of her dead grandmother find themselves in the middle of various murder investigations. Danger and hilarity ensues as the crazy duo follow the clues to discover the killers.

The Tri-Town Murders

(Small town contemporary cozies)

Follow newspaper reporter Tilly and her group of
fun, quirky friends as they solve murders in a
fictional, small town in California.

ABOUT THE AUTHOR

USA Today bestselling author Carly Winter writes fun, small town cozy mysteries, always with a dash of humor and quirky characters. When not writing, you can find her spending time with her family, on a Pilates reformer or enjoying the fantastic Arizona weather (except summer - she doesn't like summer). She does like dogs, wine and chocolate and wishes Christmas happened twice a year.

To be notified of new releases, book recommendations, to learn more about Carly and for your chance to win giveaways, please visit: CarlyWinterCozyMysteries.com